A Breakthrough Book
No. 59

The Wrong-Handed Man

Stories by
Lawrence Millman

University of Missouri Press
Columbia, 1988

University of Missouri Press, Columbia, Missouri 65211
Printed and bound in the United States of America

Library of Congress Cataloging-in-Publication Data
Millman, Lawrence.
    The wrong-handed man.
      (A Breakthrough book ; no. 59)
      I. Title. II. Series.
PS3563.I42284W76   1988   813'.54   87-27200
ISBN 0-8262-0674-3 (alk. paper)

Some of the stories in this collection originally appeared
in the following magazines: "The Wrong-Handed
Man," *Boston Review;* "Nightrangers," *Crazyhorse;* "The
Preserved Woman" and "The Triumph of Literacy,"
Crescent Review; "The Standing Stone," *The Journal of
Irish Literature;* "Prudence," "The Great Snake Mas-
sacre," "The Pickling of Rewt Chaney," "The Laying On
of Hands," and "Midnight at the Dump," *Seacoast Life;*
and "Annie Bardwell Gets Back Her Cutlery,"
TriQuarterly.

The author would like to thank the Ludwig Vogelstein
Foundation for support during part of the writing of
this book.

The publication of this book has been supported by a
grant from the National Endowment for the Arts.

For Dan, Zelma, and Barbara

Contents

The Preserved Woman

The town of Loudon Falls was starved for a good woman. Oh, it had Molly Billingsly, who was far too old, and Pumpkin Anson, who was far too generous, and it had a few drunk and miserable squaws who turned up one day after the Southport Indian Reservation collapsed into the sea during a winter storm. But the good women, they pulled up their stakes at the very first opportunity and headed down the coast. Soon even the bad women got to be pretty scarce. Dull listless eyes—the same eyes, men's eyes, boys' eyes, darksome children's eyes—greeted the traveler from every window. Then Madeline Corrigal was discovered. She was six feet one inches tall in her bare feet and had a wasp waist and her hair set in a neat bun, and she must have been some beauty in her day. Barney Ames dug her up in his blueberry bog.

As Loudon Falls neither had nor desired nor could afford a law enforcement officer, Barney took the news of his find to Armand Anson, the selectman.

How long do you think she's been dead? Armand inquired.

Oh, I'd say a hunnerd years or more.

She isn't all decomposed?

Not in the places I've looked. There's worse looking women walking around in Ellsworth and married, too . . .

I guess it's that acidy bogwater. Keeps a body good as new. Better than embalming fluid, that stuff.

A check of the town records showed that the woman was Madeline Corrigal, who died for love in the year 1871. A traveling salesman arrived in the district and courted her. Seeded her and left her, poor girl. When she saw she was to become a mother, she was so overcome by shame that she killed herself. Took a dose of rat poison. For this she was buried in unconsecrated ground. And there she lay, preserved in the bog, her resting place unmarked and her sad tale forgotten. Until now.

Well, said Armand. We don't need the state coming up here

1

and making all kinds of ruckus. Who knows what filth they'd unearth? My advice to you, Barney, is just keep quiet. Don't tell a soul about her.

Barney nodded. He was a naturally reticent man and it was no difficult matter for him to keep quiet about Madeline. Armand himself only told his daughter Pumpkin. Pumpkin was the town pump, acne-ridden and shapeless and under the age of consent though she was. Few parts of her were as loose as her lips.

After seeing Armand, Barney went home and covered up the woman with bog. To him it was like she didn't exist anymore. He could care less about women. But for Madeline Corrigal, it would be her last night on a century of calm. Next morning Barney was driving fenceposts on his back forty, and he happened to glance up and there was Edge Boatwright excavating away at his bog. He hastened over to where Edge—the town dowser—was shoveling soil right and left in a kind of frenzy.

Looking for a well, Edge?

Edge said he couldn't control his curiosity. He had to come and see the preserved woman. That's what he called her. That's what Pumpkin Anson had called her. The preserved woman. A woman taller than any man, better looking than any female you'd see on the streets in Ellsworth, silver ringlets in her ears, feet pointed and delicate like slippers.

Well, I suppose I oughter show you then. As you've made the trip all the way out here. An' so you won't be carryin' back tales about silver ringlets and beauty contests . . . Barney threw back the dirt till Madeline lay exposed in all her glory to Edge's goggly eyes.

Jesus Baldheaded Christ! the dowser gasped. I can't rightly fathom if she's the most beautiful thing I've ever seen or the ugliest.

The rat poison, Barney said. It messes up the innerds, but it keeps the outside pure.

Rat poison?

Yep. She killed herself for love.

Edge went on staring like it was the peepshow at the Fryeburg Fair. When Barney decided the man had had enough, he tossed the dirt back over Madeline. Much obliged, Edge said. On his face was a look of visible pleasure.

Quickly, with Pumpkin's help and Edge's, Madeline Corrigal became legend around Loudon Falls. Neighbor told neighbor about her, and with each telling she took on a new character. She was an old-timey free-love advocate who lived on rats and died of an overdose of them. Or she was not real at all but manufactured from a mass of molding clay by—who? Rewt Stringer? He liked to create strange sculptures in his yard from auto parts. Or she was a Negress—her skin *did* have a rather darkish hue—who died of loneliness in these light-skinned parts. Someone said she wasn't dead at all but in a deep coma and told Johnny Cope to put his lips against hers and see if she didn't turn into a princess. Now Johnny Cope was a little soft in the head. And he hadn't yet been so lucky as to kiss a woman—only goats and a few heifers and his brother lost-at-sea's gravestone. Right away he fell in love with Madeline though he didn't know her from Adam's off ox.

From their decayed colonials, their tarpaper shacks, from out of the very woodwork, folks emerged and they headed for Barney's to dig the woman up. First, like Edge Boatwright, they were only curious. Then they began to come for the sport of it, young and old alike.

Hey Hank. Me an' some of the fellows are goin' down to have a look at the preserved woman. Why don't you come an' join us?

Well, I promised the boy I'd take him fishing . . .

Bring him along instead. It'll be an education for him . . .

A few of these visitors would dig Madeline up, gaze on her for a bit, and bury her right back again, same place. Most of them, however, would leave her fully exposed to the noonday sun. By now Barney was getting a little ruffled. On a decent Saturday afternoon, his blueberry bog would resemble a football gridiron after a game. It did no good to bury her in another part of the bog. They always managed to find her again. Barney figured that they posted a sentry somewhere. One day he caught Johnny Cope with Madeline in his arms, kissing her wildly, his eyes all hope and enthusiasm. That was the last straw as far as he was concerned. He could tolerate the invasion from town no longer. He cuffed Johnny across the ear and told him to go home.

She's still the same, Johnny whimpered. She ain't no princess.

Get on home, boy. You're trespassing.

Maybe I ain't kissed her enough . . .

Here now. You're stepping all over my berries.

You only want her for yourself, the boy pouted.

You got the squirts, boy. Get out of my field or I'll see you buried here yourself. Go on, scat. At last the halfwit got the message and took off pell-mell and rackergaited for home.

Barney hoisted Madeline up over his shoulder, like she was either plunder or a wedding partner. She wasn't very heavy. Barney found he could hold her and cross the blueberry plain at a steady trot. He intended to bury her where she wouldn't be subject to Saturday afternoon sports. He settled on an area near his workshed, safeguarded from prying eyes by the shed itself as well as his house. The first time he dug, he struck rock. He moved over several feet and struck rock again. This ground would not accommodate a burial unless he blasted, and he couldn't blast without the whole town knowing about it. So he took her around back where the soil ran deeper, set her down gently, and commenced digging again. But he halted almost immediately. He was no more than ten feet from the privy. It wouldn't be fair to the woman, interring her next to a privy.

You might say he was beginning to take a proprietary interest in Madeline. Just like she was a crop of blueberries, he wanted to keep her out of harm's way. But he couldn't very well take her back to the bog and lay her with the blueberries. And it appeared that he couldn't bury her next to the house, either. Like many a man in his predicament, Barney merely reached into his pocket for a wad of snuff. He inserted the snuff between his gum and lip, then let his mind go completely blank, the better to ambush a passing thought.

Now Barney Ames was only a poor turdknocker. He wouldn't have recognized wealth if it bit him on the left testicle. He always kept his sights set low as the lowbush blueberry that he grew, cultivated, pruned, and picked. At that level he could spot a tussock moth at thirty paces. He could sniff out gray mold blight or powdery mildew a mile away. But Jesus Smuttynosed Christ, it was a pauper's life! Barney thought of all the people crowding his plain for a look-see at Madeline. If only he could put up a fence and turnstile and charge admission . . . Then he had a brainstorm. Turning to Madeline, he chuckled: You an' me's gonna make some money, sweetkins . . .

The woman, she showed no interest at all. And the way she smelled, even money would have given her a wide berth. Barney wanted to attract customers, not flies. So he got himself a bucket of bogwater and gave her leathery body a good washing. Something came off in his hand, a flap of skin or old clothing, hard to tell. But she did look better all scrubbed and clean. And she smelled less like a rotten mattress than like the earth from whence she came.

Next Barney headed into town and asked Rewt Stringer for a big glass case with a sliding door. He handed Rewt the specifications. And make it airtight, he said.

Credit?

I expect a bumper crop this year, said Barney with a smile.

Several hours later he was driving back with the case tied tight to his pickup. He paused by his mailbox and beside it he put a placard that read:

SEE THE FAMOUS PRESERVED WOMAN OF WASHINGTON COUNTY
ONLY 25 CENTS (CHEAP)

He stepped back and scratched the stubble on his chin. Squinted. He was not a whole lot satisfied. Madeline Corrigal had been a good woman, and a good woman should be worth more. Barney crossed out the 25 cents and wrote 50 cents on the placard. That was better. He didn't feel like he was shortchanging her now.

In the beginning, business wasn't bad. Hosy Cutwell came, and he hadn't been seen all year; many took him for dead, in fact, till the prospect of Madeline coaxed him out. Milt (The Real) McCoy, who raised turkeys, put in an appearance; likewise Turkey Bigelow, who torched his barn but ended up burning down his house and wife instead; Edge Boatwright twice; Josh Applegate, the manure-broker; Mem Bragdon, who distilled rotgut by the light of the moon; the Billingsly twins, Mort and Mack, hale and hearty in their ninetieth year; and the local Congregationalist minister, Mr. Ashley.

Ezra Adams, the undertaker, brought his whole family. He took a professional interest in Madeline. He gazed at her admiringly. Couldn't do a better job myself, he said.

It really wasn't me, Barney told him. It's just that she's a natural . . . And he looked with pride at the glassed-in woman. She was seated on a large blueberry crate with her hands folded demurely in her lap. In those hands he had placed a lily. He had combed her hair as best he could and wrapped a shawl that had been his mother's over her shoulders. All in all, she seemed quite comfortable. A person might even have construed on her ancient lips the makings of a smile.

And then, of course, Johnny Cope came. The town albatross. Only a matter of time before he showed up. Barney winced. Sorry, Johnny, he said. Only paying customers . . .

Johnny Cope grinned a great, beaming, full-mouthed grin. He emptied his pockets into Barney's hands: a dead fieldmouse, a fishhook, a moist hanky, a spent shotgun shell, and a return ticket stub from the State Farm. God's plenty. Johnny allowed as how he was the payingest customer of all.

The boy was so eager, Barney let him enter the house. And enter he did, embracing Madeline's glass case with the full-bodied hug of an octopus. Barney had to restrain him. Now you just sit down here, he said, pulling up a chair. And Johnny sat in front of his lady love eyeing her the whole livelong day. Ever so often, he'd mumble cryptic things to her in his idiot tongue. Barney vowed not to let him come back. The genuine customers would object to him. *He* objected to him. The boy gave him the creepy-crawlies staring like that. And so when Johnny returned the next day and held out a dead sparrow and an old Canadian Pacific Railway menu, Barney barred the door.

Hey Barney Ames. I want to see my princess.

She ain't yours, Barney said. She's mine. An' you better not pester me anymore 'less you got four bits.

I want to see her.

Barney answered him by waving his 30–30 Winchester out the window. Your carcass better be outa here by the count of three, he said. One, two . . . And he exploded with laughter watching Johnny light out hell-bent and crooked across the field.

Toward the end of the week his business trailed off. Only a few lowdown and morose-looking gents from the barrel-hoop factory across the county stopped in to see the preserved woman. They peered at her and then departed without a word. Afterward Barney discovered that one of them had left a couple of iron washers in the till. Another put in a token that permitted the bearer two meals for the price of one at a defunct diner. Real lowdowns, Barney thought.

What had happened? He met Edge Boatwright practicing his dowsing beside the town water supply. He asked him what the explanation was for Madeline's sudden decline in popularity.

Edge said: My guess is, it has to do with that Pumpkin Anson girl. She's startin' to charge for her favors. It's all folks can do to come up with the money. She's got 'em on all fours, so she does. They don't have anything left over for your preserved woman.

Pumpkin Anson's flatter'n a pair of pieplates. Folks *pay* for her?

Sure do. Church collection yestidy was next to nothing. Saturday's her big night, I hear.

Christmas, what a world!

Yeah, an' I believe she got the idea for charging from your own little operation, fellow . . .

Barney spat out his snuff. He was ashamed to hang his hat in a town where a Pumpkin Anson could outdraw a good woman like Madeline Corrigal. His shame forced him to lower his asking price to 25 cents a visit. He even decided to launch a Pay Later Plan. His placard advertised family rates. But there were no takers. Madeline could have been lying neglected and forlorn in her bog for all the interest the fickle town now took in her.

And Barney's troubles still weren't over. One day Rewt Stringer drove up in his Studebaker-Packard-Dodge pickup mix. He said he needed the money right away. Else he'd have to repossess the glass case.

Don't got it, Rewt. Wait till berry season's underway.

Sorry, old pal. Jem Bragdon wants a phone booth for his store and this is as good a casing as any, I'm thinking. Now, would you mind removing *that*?

Barney knew better than to argue with a man who was the town tax collector. So he removed the offending body and helped Rewt load the case into the pickup. Before he drove off, Rewt mentioned an odor strong enough to flatten a bull elephant.

The preserved woman did seem to be less preserved than before. Barney decided to carry her back to her original resting place. This he did with a twinge of regret. All his moneymaking plans had come to naught.

A couple of days later, a foreigner from Massachusetts pulled up in front of the house, flashed his press card, said he was a newspaperman. He wanted to photograph the preserved woman for his paper. He was willing to offer ten dollars for the privilege. Needless to say, Barney jumped at the offer. With this kind of publicity, he might be able to compete with Pumpkin Anson. He might even be able to corner the out-of-state market, which Pumpkin could never do. Pumpkin was at best a local attraction. Madeline was universal, a woman for the whole world to see and admire.

Briskly he set out with the newsman across his blueberry plain. They reached the spot where he had buried the woman. As the man stood poised with his camera, Barney heaved up shovelful after shovelful of bog. He dug to a depth of five feet, but Madeline Corrigal was nowhere to be seen. She'd gone and vanished on him! Flustered, he couldn't stop digging. Maybe he was mistaken about where he buried her. But he knew he couldn't be mistaken about a thing like that. He knew this bog like he knew his own face. At last the newspaperman coughed. Said he hadn't come all the way up here just to watch a man dig a new cellar hole.

She ain't where I put her, Barney shrugged.

The man called the whole story a hoax and drove away in a huff.

I'll get her back for you, Barney yelled after him. He dashed into the house and phoned up Armand Anson and told him that he'd been robbed. The selectman seemed to be in one of his dour, legalistic moods. He said: Strictly speaking, Barney, she isn't your property at all. Not at all. She belongs to the government.

The government?

Right. If you found, say, buried treasure on your property, the U. S. of A. has a claim on 60 percent of it. The rest is yours. But as this preserved woman can't be divided, being a person separate and entire, the U. S. of A. owns the whole lot of her outright. And it chooses—through me, its lawful representative—not to conduct an investigation as to the woman's whereabouts. Sorry, old poke. See you at bingo tomorrow evening.

Barney cursed the man under his breath. He figured that Armand was in cahoots with his daughter. Pleased as punch to have a monopoly on the local business now. Lord knows what rake-offs he was getting from Pumpkin. You're not going to see that woman's like again, leastways around here, he remarked to the selectman, and the blue dolefuls were in his voice.

*   *   *

Now a few folks said it was the exposure that finally got the best of Madeline Corrigal. She'd been dug up too much, she'd seen too much sun, and her antiquated system couldn't take it. Proverbial decay snatched her, they said, and ground her to dust in practically no time.

Others were less sure. Ezra Adams claimed she was put on display at some fair or freak show where she'd be more widely appreciated than she was in the town of Loudon Falls. Edge Boatwright heard that she had made it to the mummy division of the State Museum and he planned to visit her first chance he got. No, impossible, someone told him. All that manhandling had forced her out of her coma like a butterfly from its cocoon and she just rose up and walked off, just like that, left her bogland to seek her fortune elsewhere. Turkey Bigelow agreed. He had observed her or a woman very much like her, a tall woman and brownskinned, hitting up strangers for meal money in Ellsworth. Held for ransom! declared Roger Holly. Hell, no! Local hooligans got her, tore her to shreds and fed the pieces to the gulls. Even a few people claimed it was Johnny Cope who did it, stole her and hid her so he could have her all to himself. Johnny was looking unusually blissful of late, like at last he'd managed to turn her into the princess of his dreams.

Whatever happened to Madeline, it was a given fact that Barney Ames never had a decent stand of blueberries again. If they came up at all, the berries would be bitter and withered and hardly fit for the hogs, every last one of them. The leaves would always be wilted and black like a hard frost had hit them. But no frost ever hit those parts in the middle of summer. It was all highly mysterious. Barney almost felt like something vital, some nutrient or other, had been sucked out of his soil.

Annie Bardwell Gets Back Her Cutlery

Though he died in his sleep of ordinary old age, the rumor persisted that Grandpa Sawyer died trying to satisfy his housekeeper Annie Bardwell in bed. That no-good slut, people said. The Sawyer son who descended on the estate, a sporting-goods retailer in Concord, told Annie he'd bring her to court for trespass if she ever showed her pockmarked face around there again. Tearfully she asked for her cutlery. She had brought it over from Millbrook Farm twelve years ago. She and Grandpa had eaten with it nearly every night. "Get the hell out of my house," the son told her. So, suitcase in hand, she began walking through the fir and hemlock forest, along the old tote road, back to the farm.

Annie, at forty, hadn't lost the taut muscularity that had first struck Grandpa with such lust. Her long, tapered thighs still revealed youthful patternings of muscle and bone, and her high breasts still brought men's eyes down from her face. The trouble, of course, lay with this face. At age eight she had contracted German measles. The local doctor was in the middle of a bout with Christian Science, and he instructed Annie's father to "have faith, just believe those measles will melt away and they'll do it." George Bardwell was never renowned for his faith; he was much better at training gundogs and driving fence posts, with the result that Annie's face was left with a jumble of pits, ruts, and small craters. She knew this testimony to the wonders of Christian healing would never leave her. It was a whole year before she could look at herself in the mirror.

Only Grandpa could tolerate her face, but he was dead. Now she had nowhere to go but home, where her brother Clarence still lived. The years she had been with Grandpa, she had kept herself out of touch with Clarence. Grandpa thought he was crude. All she knew for certain about him was his accident: a chain saw leaping back suddenly and slicing his arm off like it was made of rubber. She had sent him the nicest "Get Well" card she could find. And Grandpa had covered the hospital expenses, for Clarence never was and never would be insured.

Annie wasn't in any rush to get back. Once she rested for an hour or so on the warm needles beneath a balsam fir. Ten feet above her she saw the black face of a porcupine. She stared up at the animal for the longest time, and it just lay there in the crotch of the tree, its sullen face watching, waiting.

She knew the farm would be a desolation. She knew Clarence could not have managed the upkeep all on his own. And she guessed he'd sold off the cattle to support his boozing. Boozing? With Clarence it was more like a way of life. At fourteen he'd sneak off into one of the cowsheds with a six-pack. Or if he feared detection, he'd light out for the sugarhouse in the maple wood, making Annie promise not to tell. But mostly Papa did find out, perhaps because of his own fondness for liquor. And beat Clarence as he did, trimming the boy's lean backside with belts, harnesses, or whatever paraphernalia happened to be handy, he only succeeded in driving him deeper into drink. The beatings continued until Clarence was twenty and Papa died of a rotten liver, going crazy first and writing letters to a favorite gundog that had been dead for eight years.

The shortcut through the woods brought the distance between Grandpa's place and Millbrook Farm down to less than five miles. Annie came out near the sugarhouse, where only a few dying maples hid among the evergreens, gnarled, falling, riddled with fungus. Lifting her skirt, she picked her way through what had once been a meadow but now was bogged up by a beaver dam. On higher ground, the pasture was beginning to revert to second-growth saplings.

Ahead, the barn showed itself to be in tumbledown condition, sagging on its north side as if a great weight had fallen there; the barnyard was a litter of old milking pails, cutterbars, and barrel hoops. Papa's half-ton Chevrolet truck—an engineless, wheelless, seatless hulk—was three-quarters buried by the earth, and beside it was Clarence's own pickup, in not much better shape, with only a few random splotches of the original blue peering through the red rust. The old boards of the house itself, as Annie expected, were unpainted and nail-sprung.

She rattled at the door. Locked. Clarence's pickup was in the yard, so he must be home. She went around to the back of the house, past the cellar hole into which the upper part of the chimney had toppled. The back door was slightly ajar, trembling ever so gently from a breeze. Without knocking, she entered. There at the table, pint bottles of whiskey all around him like chess pieces, sat Clarence poring over a girlie magazine.

"Clarence!"

"Annie . . ."

"I came . . . came through the woods."

"You're back."

"I'm back."

She gazed down at this gaunt one-armed man, her brother. He was wearing just an undershirt, a bag of ash-gray flannel that sagged from his chest. Thin as he had been in the old days, he was even thinner now. Like a hayrake. He looked like he hadn't eaten in the whole twelve years.

"They said you'd been booted out. They said it was that little knob of a sheep's turd Buddy Sawyer done it."

"Buddy, he ain't so bad . . ."

"Christ but he didn't feel the same way about you."

"Well, it was his house. It became his house. He could have done far worse to me."

"Yeah. He could have fed you to his hogs."

"Buddy don't keep hogs, Clarence. He's got himself a store in Concord."

"It's just an expression, that's all. Feed you to the hogs. You ain't heard that before?"

She fell to a shy silence. Then Clarence said: "Well, set down your suitcase. You look silly just standing there, like some sort of salesman."

Annie put down her suitcase.

"Kinda warming up a little," Clarence said. He swigged from one of the whiskey bottles.

"A little."

"Black flies'll be out soon. Like to collect all those little buggers in a bag and dump them in the river."

"Mosquitoes, too."

"Right . . ."

All of a sudden Annie grabbed his wrist, a wrist almost more slender than her own, and shaking it, she said: "That Buddy has kept all our cutlery. All our silver. Mama's dowry that she brought over from Lancaster. Kept it like it was his own. You think that's right?"

"That old man leave you any money? Did he leave you anything?"

"I don't know, Clarence. But that cutlery, it's been in the family forever and ever . . ."

"Forever and ever," he mimicked, shaking his wrist free from her grasp. "But forever don't matter. Nothing matters. Tableware. Cattle. Hay crop. Mowing. Raking. Baling. Hauling. Believe this matters, though." He held up a whiskey bottle and cracked a grin full of tooth-black. Eyes tightly shut, his head jerked fowlwise, and down in his face came dark unshorn hair all hung in clots like a sheep's scut. Drunk, she thought. It's just like old times. And she poured a small glass of her own.

"That's right, girl," he said. "You have to help yourself around here."

"They shuh got a lot of liquor at the Sawyer place," she said, draining her glass.

"I bet they do."

"Wine. That's what we had with just about every meal. Can you imagine?"

"You can't get much of a hum off wine. Quiet stuff."

". . . and whiskey like you never seen. Johnny Walker Red Label. Row after row of it."

They sat silently in each other's company. Annie tried to accustom herself to the absence of an arm where an arm should have been. She watched Clarence's face—a face deep and pensive, as if mindful of an infinity of liquor; a boyish face frozen into a mask of furrows and age. A soft breeze swept through the room, rustling the magazine pages into glimpses of disembodied breasts and thighs. At last she blurted out, "They scorn us so, Clarence. They scorn us so."

"I know, girl. Think I don't know?"

"Jack Sawyer—that's a nephew—he said you wa'n't no better than a shack person. Said someone should try and get you to sell out, so's they could turn the place into a hunting lodge."

He went to the broom closet and brought out his Winchester.

Then he regarded her with barbed-wire eyes. "I'll blast their balls all the way to Boston. Christ, I will!"

It was with Clarence standing there that Annie could see how thin he really was. Maybe it was the missing arm, but he didn't seem to be much more than the bare bones of a skeleton. She decided her brother needed food. Needed flesh to stretch over those exposed bones. She would see to it that his stomach was full. Grandpa always said it was a wealthy man who took a full stomach to bed.

She began searching high and low for food. In one cupboard, she located the blackened carcass of a partridge or woodcock hung on a hook. In another, only salt and pepper shakers, both empty, with the inscriptions "I'm fulla S" and "I'm fulla P." (Papa, she recalled, would nearly double up with laughter when he asked her to pass one of these shakers.) The pickling jars were threaded together by spiderwebs; in one of them a dead mouse lay stretched out on the remains of, she guessed, tomatoes. The bread box housed a motley of screwdrivers and drill bits.

There didn't appear to be a single edible morsel in the whole kitchen. She was about ready to give up when she opened a drawer and discovered a Wheaties box among a scattering of shotgun shells. For the moment she felt like she had won a small victory against impossible odds. Now all she needed was milk, which instinct told her she would find in this house, of all houses. She was mistaken; Clarence must have sold off the last of the cows. Yet it hardly mattered, since the Wheaties box contained nothing but shotgun shells. In frustration, she began to cry.

"Don't turn on the Niagara around me. I can't stand it." Clarence offered her a stained handkerchief that smelled of crankcase oil.

"But Clarence, you can't be eating. There's not a thing in the house and you're just so thin. You bothered about eating at all? Say you're eating something?"

"Miss Busybody . . ."

Disgust fairly leapt from his face. He stood up again and went out the back, pausing as he left to say: "You know why that front door is locked? Know why? Social workers. They're thicker than fiddlers in hell. Come here to tell me I can't live like this or I can't live like that. Say I should learn me a trade, go to night school. Shit in a bucket, they're just as bad as those Sawyers! Next time one of them jolterheads comes for a visit, I'll blow his balls to Boston, too! If there's one thing I can't stomach, it's a busybody."

Annie smiled through her tears. Her brother's tongue was as sharp as ever. He could still vent his spleen with the best of them. She recalled the time twenty years ago when the New York lawyer had driven up in his big Plymouth sedan. Papa, dying, wanted to sell the farm for a song, but Clarence so insulted the man, calling him names like "wicked Jew" and "sidewinding sonafabitch," that he just turned around and drove back to New York in a huff. "He takes us for country jakes," her brother said. That was the last time Papa whipped him.

Clarence returned with a greasy duck-sack and dumped it on the kitchen table. Out came a torrent of dead animals: a skunk, a raccoon in a rind of blood, a fox, squirrels, and a monster jackrabbit, one big eye wrinkled and black, punctured by buckshot. Annie watched while a loop of putty-colored intestine slowly eased from the underside of the skunk.

Her brother's eyes sparkled; they seemed piercing enough to freeze the flies that now hovered over the table.

"Ever seen this much around that rich man's across the way?"

"Clarence, that man loved me . . ."

"All decent grub except maybe the fox, which is got mange. Coon's been run over. It's dinner. The others I shot yesterday. Can shoot just as good with one arm as two. And this sack don't tell half the story. I get deer, poach them whenever I like. Used to jack them, but no Fish and Game man's been around for years. Porcupines. Woodchucks. Rabbits. The odd moose. I don't go out nowadays without double-aught buckshot in my belt. Not been to a supermarket in two years. No need to."

"But don't you think these creatures, they're not fit . . . not fit to . . . ?"

But she knew better than to tell him about the meals at Grandpa's. Steak, always the best of steak, twice a week; fresh fish from Littleton; and huge heaping plates of greens.

"A man gets older," Clarence said, "he finds there're lots of foods he can do just as well without. All them canned foods, for instance. They just turn your insides to mush and you wake up one morning feeling soft as cowshit. That won't afflict me, girl."

There was an odd intensity in his face as his lank and corded hand shoved all the animals but the bloodstained raccoon back in the sack. Annie thought: He enjoys these animals, actually enjoys them, enjoys the touch and feel and smell of them. And as she gazed at him, what she took to be his delight spread naturally to her. All at once she felt quite close to him. She felt like touching him. She wanted to press her cheek to his cheek, to show him that all these years at Grandpa's hadn't made her cold to him. She wanted to tell him, yes, we must eat what the Lord provides. If He chooses to bless us with raccoon or even porcupine, then we must be grateful. Many folks don't even have that. But she was so weary from her tramp through the woods, all she could manage was a weak smile. She closed her eyes and fell asleep right there at the table, and in a dream she was scraping flattened raccoon bodies off the road with a big broad spatula.

*   *   *

Later she awakened alone in a kitchen half-tinted with darkness. From the window she could see the sun slip down, yellow and dying, over the hills of Vermont. Clarence was not around. He couldn't tolerate me being such a busybody, she thought to herself.

The raccoon was still on the table. Even in death its bandit face still flinched. The caved shape gave off a slight reek, which mingled with the stronger reek of Clarence's sweat. Annie guessed she was meant to skin and dress the creature, a task she was in no hurry to accomplish. So she decided to find out what disasters had befallen the house since Clarence had become its sole occupant. She headed first for the parlor, her mother's place of refuge when Papa was drunk. George Bardwell had tended to treat his wife like she was a breechy cow, not really clouting her but slapping her around a bit. Yet he would never follow her into the parlor for fear of breaking one of her plates or glasses. Jennie Bardwell always swore that if her husband so much as chipped a sliver off her crystal, she would nail him with his own shotgun.

Now as she stood by the door, Annie could see that the parlor had been turned into a workroom. There was a cellary damp odor in the air. The davenport was stacked with old and presumably dead batteries. A V-8 engine sat in its own oil on the rug (worn down, she noticed, to its essential warp and woof). The engine appeared to be partially dismantled and then forgotten. How typical of Clarence. She stepped into an ocean of wrenches, crowbars, mauls, chisels, shaves, burnishers, calipers, hammers, and a Hudson Bay ax; she stepped lightly and made her way to the cabinet, inside which she could see the flowered plates and crystal untouched since she left—a strange, enduring presence in the midst of all these tools. On the shelf below, however, only dust lay upon what for ages had been the home of her mother's cutlery.

She couldn't remember a time when her mother had ever used the cutlery. Waxing and polishing, holding it at arm's length to admire the finish, Jennie always told her daughter that she was saving it for a special occasion. But special occasions were as rare at Millbrook Farm as three-headed calves. Through Annie's childhood the silver sat on display in the parlor cabinet, polished to a mirrorlike brilliance yet as idle as Grandpa's antique oven peel. A few weeks before she died—of what no one precisely knew, perhaps leukemia—her mother called Annie to her bed and said: "You're not very smart and God only knows you're ugly as sin, but maybe, if you're lucky, some man will take pity on you and marry you. And then you can bring the cutlery to his house as I brought it to your father's."

With her mother dead, Papa began to—what was the right word for it?—"bother" her. He'd finger the curve of her breast where it nestled inside her fuzzy sweater, telling her what a big girl she was now, what a pretty girl. "I ain't nowhere near pretty, Papa," she informed him (though she was grateful for any compliment). "Oh, I don't mean your face," he said. "I don't mean your face at all." She remembered that warm evening when he pulled her aside in one of the cow cribs. He'd been baling since noon and the summery scent of hay lay heavy all over him. "You're my honey," he said. He slid his hand roughly along the inside of her thigh. And she told him, "I want to marry you, Papa. I want to bring you all that nice cutlery. Mama's cutlery. I want it to be yours forever and ever." At her words, he pulled his hand away abruptly. Whatever thoughts moiled in his head didn't come out. He just walked off, leaving her seated on a milk pail. She felt like she was dead. There'd never be anyone else interested in her as long as she lived. She was already twelve years old. She would die a foul-tempered old maid; the cutlery would be intact in the family parlor to her last living day.

Now the hummocky slopes behind the house were fading quickly in the dusk. It was time to attend the raccoon. Back in the darkened kitchen, she could scarcely make out a thing. She flicked the light switch on and off a few times without bringing the room to light. Then she tried the switch in the hallway with the same result. The house had no electricity. That had to be why she hadn't heard the familiar sound of the shallow-well pump clinking and hissing. Clarence must not have paid his electricity bills. Come to think of it, she really couldn't imagine Clarence paying a bill. Such was her brother—he couldn't tolerate busybodies.

Annie groped around for a kerosene lamp. In the larder her hand recoiled with a jolt from the dead hairy head of some animal. She went to the stairwell.

"Clarence!" she yelled. "Clarence, I got to have a kerosene lamp."

He didn't answer. He was probably outside. As she stepped out of the house, a bat flew past her, fluttering silently and swiftly through its angular courses, barely missing her head. Only the gray ghosts of the barn and cowsheds could be seen through the darkness.

"Clarence, I got to have some light," she shouted in the direction of the barn.

Still no answer. Then she noticed that Clarence's pickup was not in its usual place next to Papa's derelict truck. Her brother must have driven off while she was still asleep. Annie walked and ruminated and absently furrowed the dust of the barnyard with her foot. Had she been so irksome that she drove her brother off into the night? Was she too much of a busybody? She tried to recall what curious questions she had asked that might have grated on his person. She had steered clear of his missing arm or the ruination of the farm. She guessed that she was just a nuisance, a nuisance plain and simple; that was all.

On the back steps Annie sat down and wrapped her arms around her legs, resting her head on the arch of her knees. She clung to herself like this for some time—perhaps an hour, perhaps two. She did not move except once when a broad-tailed hawk's sorrowful whistle made her look up toward the night sky.

At last she saw the headlights—two pinhole eyes growing bigger and bigger as they scudded down the road. In front of them a phantom rabbit froze in an attitude of surprise and then vanished in the dark. The pickup rattled along until it reached the house. Then, with a grate of shifting gears and a spastic sucking noise, the motor died, hushed abruptly in the stillness of the night. The door swung open and Clarence hopped out.

"Clarence, please may I have some light for the kitchen?"

He ignored her. "Help me unload, will you?"

She went around to the rear of the truck. There she saw a number of cases of Johnny Walker Red Label.

"Hey!" she exclaimed.

"First time I ever done the Sawyer place," Clarence said. "You wa'n't telling tales, girl. I got a Christly harvest there. Keep us happy till Judgment Day."

"You stole this whiskey from the Sawyer place?"

"Shuh did. Done nearly every house worth doing around here at one time or another. Think I'd go to the State Liquor Store? Place is too costly for a poor pumpkin roller like me."

Despite herself, Annie looked with affection at this haul of Grandpa's favorite whiskey, snatched from his own store of liquor at the house.

"I left the wine," Clarence said. "Give them something to drink when they come back Saturday. Folks that only live in a house weekends, they deserve to have their liquor raided."

"I bet the police catch up with you," she said. "I just bet they do."

"Nah, never. You see, I drink the evidence." And he made a throaty laugh, his swollen coddle-egg eyes dancing.

They put the first batch on the kitchen floor.

"Clarence, will you kindly say if you got some kind of lamp around here?"

"Keep the lamps hid," he told her. "Those social worker fellows threaten to take them off me. Fearful I might set the house afire if I get too stewed. Can you imagine?" He rummaged briefly in the high cupboard. Soon a match was struck and the image of lamp flame was skittering on the ceiling.

"How do they expect you to see in the dark?" Annie said. She had a vision of her brother, deprived of his kerosene lamps, flailing about from room to darkened room, as outside the house an army of social workers stood with arms folded and superior grins on their faces.

They had just finished with the last of the cases when Clarence, reaching into the front seat, said: "Almost forgot. I brought back the cutlery."

The cutlery! She grabbed the velvety box with eager hands, fondled it for a moment, and then undid the clasp, counting—yes, the soupspoons, the pickle fork, the gravy ladle, the butter knives, and in the middle, yes, the big knife that had carved twelve Thanksgiving turkeys and twelve Christmas hams. They were all here, every last one of them, here in their pride.

Nothing could have brought her greater joy or brought her closer to her brother. Gooseflesh spread along her shoulders and arms and downward. She leaned forward and pressed his lips with a lingering kiss, which he met with a kiss of his own. She began to sigh as he clutched her body, clutched her breasts. Then he stopped as if in panic.

"I'm pisspoor," he said in a low voice. "Arm's gone, body's all gone to pieces. You wouldn't hardly want to touch me. You wouldn't, really."

"It's all right," she said. "I don't mind. We're blood."

The Triumph of Literacy

Ruppert Flower, Jr., of Center Wrexham was slated to deliver Molly Bloom's Soliloquy during the annual Pentasquam County All-Joyce Festival. But Ruppert had to be scratched a week before the festival because he came down with a bad case of the nuptial blues and shot his wife Nellie while Henry Perkins the tax assessor was loving her up. Ruppert shot Henry, too. And for good measure he shot Henry's sheepdog Lycidas. The authorities sent him to the State Prison to cool his heels for a spell.

Meanwhile, the good folks who organized the festival were beset by a dilemma. Rupe had delivered that soliloquy ever since the festival was first spawned. And he'd grown in the part just as the festival itself had grown from a mere applejack tipple to an all-county literary extravaganza. In the early stages, he'd been a bit rugged—points off a week or so and a hardscrabble beard that made him look more like a patch of tundra than a lush female lying there in bed. Also, he spat Bull Durham ooze.

But Time, which wizens what it does not outright violate, was kind to Rupe's performance. At last he came to deliver the soliloquy so Christly well that not even Molly Bloom herself in all her glory could have bettered him at it. He used his Uncle Nate's army cot and a paisley chamber pot and instead of a negligee, he wore a see-through fatigue shirt that dipped clear down to his knees. Occasionally, as a personal touch, he'd lay a dead deer athwart the cot (the festival took place during hunting season).

Half the county wanted to cancel the soliloquy, in Rupe's honor, rather than consign it to some lesser luminary. Others proposed that the festival itself be removed to the State Prison, and that Rupe's cell be decked out with Bloomsday memorabilia. But the warden vetoed that right off. He said he wasn't going to see his prison turned into a celebration of Joyce. He could tolerate Jean Genet, but that Joyce really sucked the nether teat.

The local fish-and-game man said he wouldn't mind dump-

21

ing the soliloquy in favor of a seminar or two on wildlife management, with special reference to Joyce.

And Hazen Blanchard the scrap merchant thought a demolition derby with English professors might be rather amusing.

At this juncture there formed a hard-core action group comprised of lit crit beldams and lady loggers who vowed they'd fight the issue of the soliloquy even unto the state's primeval courts. They said *machismo* already had Pentasquam County by the balls. Dump the soliloquy and you might as well teach rape in the schools. Whereupon the group set out to find a new Molly:

"What about Turkey Bigelow, Em'ly? He used to do Saturday morning Beckett in the Grange."

"That was for kids. Besides, I've already asked him. He says he looks pure awful in a bra."

"Well, how 'bout Barney Cadwallader? He's written that book on postwar Commie verse. And he's one of the finest fornicators you'd ever meet. A real gentleman."

"Go on, hon. Where you been? Hookworms carried off Barney last summer."

"Well, what about his brother Hammond? You ever see Hammond drive a fence post, Em'ly? Mercy!"

"I asked him, too. But he said he wouldn't do it out of respect for Rupe. Told me we ought to replace the soliloquy with an evening of silence and prayer. Ain't that just like a man?"

And so it went. The best talents seemed to be in jail, or snackered, or dead, or too whelmed by modesty to follow in Rupe's monumental footsteps. Oscar Simpson said he'd done a bit of Jacobean tragedy in his youth, but he was too busy with his tofu-and-marigold farm to swot up Joyce on such short notice.

The action group was nearly ready to get a court-ordered injunction. But at the eleventh hour they got some heartening news which proved that the System, after all, was rather sweet. The group was so delighted that they all went out and got hotter than skunks on spiked cranapple juice.

Came the big day. Joyceans packed the fairgrounds. They heard Virgil Sprockett's homely explication "*Finnegans Wake: A Garage Mechanic's View.*" In one tent, the county's best marksmen took turns shooting at a cardboard image of Joyce moving back and forth between scaled-down models of Paris and Trieste. In another tent, there was a workshop (complete with bars of Lava soap for all the participants) on *A Portrait of the Artist* in the light of new mulching techniques. And every youngster got a free James Joyce eyepatch at the gate.

After a gala supper, folks adjourned to the First Congregationalist Church for the closing event—Molly Bloom's Soliloquy—though who would deliver it was the subject for some heated scholarly debate:

"I bet they bring in Sir John Gielgud."

"Naw. It'll be Jack Barth or one of them guys."

"Turkey Bigelow . . ."

Well, at least the prop men had come through. They'd turned the inside of the church into a replica of seedy Dublin, circa 1904. A potato sack adorned the Statue of the Blessed Virgin. The altar was bathed in a rich red light, the better to evoke Molly's boudoir. And there, next to the pulpit, was Rupe's old army cot with a dead deer lying on it.

"It's a sacrilege, a pure sacrilege," said Asa Partlow, "usin' his personals, with him in jail an' all."

Then suddenly two armed guards walked in with a handcuffed Ruppert Flower, Jr. He was arrayed in traditional prison stripes with a plunging décolletage, and he wore the Red Sox cap with which he sometimes portrayed Molly. "We love you, Rupe," someone shouted, and the rest of the audience followed with loud applause. As they reached the altar, one of the guards undid the handcuffs and made a statement to the effect that a new warden—a Structuralist and authority on Robbe-Grillet— had taken over the reins of the prison. Henceforth greater leniency would be extended to the avant-garde. Joyceans would receive special treatment. Turning to Rupe, he said, "Well, it's your show, mate . . ."

And thus began another evening of literacy in Pentasquam County.

Prudence

Now this'll be none too pleasant so it's best you stay home sweetie
Yeah you're too young kid
But she was my Aunt too
She ain't nobody's Aunt now

And then with three backfires and a grating of gears they sped off into the cold October night.

Lanie's folks treated her like she was still in her swaddling clothes. Or like she was the one, not Aunty Prudence, who'd tumbled down the steps. She felt scorned. She had as much right to attend to her Great Aunt as anyone else. She'd already gazed on the stillborn boy her sister Amy bore last Fourth of July. She'd seen Deke Otway's black retriever fished from the well after their water started to taste funny. So it wasn't as if she was any stranger to death.

Most fearful tumble I've ever seen, Doctor Tuttle of Agamenticus told them. From the top of the stairwell all the way down to the very bottom. That's a lot of stairs, Mr. Aikens. You could spend half the morning counting them. I wouldn't bring that girl if I were you . . .

Well, Lanie thought, rolling over in bed, I wouldn't bring you a lone course of sprouts if you was starving, Doctor Tuttle of Agamenticus . . .

For she wasn't afraid of her Aunt. How could a person fear a Free Will Baptist? Crushed and maimed and mangled though she might be. How could a person fear a bringer of sweets?

The woman's kisses tasted like old mayonnaise.

Mercy! but you're getting big, girl . . .
Mercy! Have I forgotten my spectacles again?

Eyelids like walnut hulls.

Smokeblue holes in the cords of her neck.

And she'd never leave her big white house in The Hollow except to visit Lanie and her sister and brothers. She'd never arrive without a fudge cake or maple creams or some sort of pie. After the stillborn boy, Aunt Pru's bounty increased tenfold.

24

One Sunday afternoon they nearly drowned in apple turnovers and brownies. Some had to be mashed into feed for the cattle.

Suddenly the curtains in Lanie's room started to sway like the white beards of patriarchs. Her wallpaper came alive with cavorting wraiths in the sharp moonlight. She jumped at the sight of her own knees shrouded in the sheet.

Now a mist was taking shape from the bed itself. It seemed to separate into legs and arms and a lean Baptist skull with Aunty Pru's nightcap on it. The face wore a wrinkly grin. It had a gray mouth which sagged open like it was getting ready to say: *Mercy . . .*

You ain't nobody's Aunt now, she told it.

Then Lanie realized she was only seeing her own breath in the chill air. She sighed. Her fearless flesh was nearly yeasty with sweat. She turned in her bed and there was a moist spot the length of her body on the sheet.

She'd have a heart attack if this kept up. They'd find her dead in her bed, her eyes popped open like she'd seen some unspeakable horror. And it would serve them right, the baboons.

She needed something to batten down her nerves. Food, perhaps. So she grabbed a lamp and lit out for the kitchen.

She loved the kitchen.

In the kitchen no harm could come to her.

Or so she believed.

She'd only just begun messing with the pancake batter when she heard footfalls crunching the gravel outside. One of the heifers called out in alarm. Then another. Lanie's throat went dry as last year's bird nests.

Someone was knocking on the front door. Then someone opened it. Clumped along the hardwood floor.

Well, Lanie thought, at least it ain't the ghost of Aunt Prudence. For the old woman never wore heavy boots. But then whose ghost could it be? Or maybe it was some tinker come for Grampa Crowley's sea chest and Papa's old muzzle-loader that he could fire with a match head and seed hulls.

"Hey Frankie. Anyone home? *Frankie!*"

She knew that voice. It was Cyril Morse's, from down the road. Then Cyril himself, a farm-bodied boy/man, walked into the kitchen. "Frankie home?" he said.

"Boy, am I glad to see you!" Lanie exclaimed. "I thought you might be a ghost . . ."

Said Cyril: "I was headed for the dump. To shoot a few rats. Figured your brother would like to come along."

She was standing there in nothing but her slip. She quickly folded her arms across her chest. "Frankie's not here," she said. "Our old Aunt fell down the stairs and broke every bone in her body. They drove up to The Hollow to see her."

"She dead?" he said.

"I guess. But they wouldn't let me go."

"And they just up and left you alone here?"

He was gazing at her like he never saw anyone in a slip before. She uncrossed her arms because maybe she was drawing too much attention to herself. His gaze did not waver.

"'Scuse me," she said. As she hurried upstairs, she glanced at herself in the mirror. Christly slip was so tight on her, she looked like a canvas sack brimming with potatoes. Cyril Morse must surely wonder at a girl who wore her own hand-me-downs.

She put on her terry-cloth robe that had pretty purple crocuses growing on it.

When Lanie came back, Cyril Morse was sitting with his feet plunked up on the table. "I never had an Aunty," he said. "'Course since I'm adopted, it's hard to tell. You mind now that she's dead?"

He wore his hair like a hedgehog's.

He brought a smell into the room not unlike hay going a little sour.

"Sure," Lanie said. "She gave us nice sweeties all the time. But she was a Baptist, you know. We're United Methodists . . ."

"Well, we're Congregationalists. But I sure wish Frankie was around. No fun shooting rats by yourself."

"I never seen fun in killing rats anyway."

Lanie didn't want him to stay nor did she want to see him leave, either. She felt protected (from whatever) with him here but also a little uncomfortable. Like he was going to rise up at any moment and start shooting dishes and plates in the pantry cupboard, in the absence of rats.

"Hey, you making pancakes?"

"Yeah."

"I'll have some, thank you. Ain't eaten since early in the morning. Our brood sow died on us. We had to keep watch on the little pigs all day. Caught one of 'em sucking on a valve stem . . ."

"How many do you want?"

"Oh, five or six, thank you. And some milk to wash them down."

"Okay."

"Sow dies on you, it's like your bank burned down. This one could throw fifteen pigs at a whack."

She had never gabbed with him at such length before. Once, at a dance, they'd exchanged a few words about the guitar player, who had a palsy. But he was Frankie's friend, not hers.

He smeared back a tousle of hair. "And some toast if you don't mind, thank you."

"Don't they feed you at home?"

"They feed me all right. But like I said, I ain't had the chance to eat. Never had a moment's peace from those little pigs."

Lanie regarded him out of the corner of her eye. She knew he sometimes went with her brother to call on the Gagnon girls, seven miles down the county road and looser than bunnies in heat. Often Frankie would not get back until the next morning.

"Those razorbacks they got down South," Cyril remarked, "I'd sure like to have a few of them. They're tough roosters that wouldn't croak on you like an old Hampshire softy."

"How come your sow croaked on you?"

"Choked on a damn apple."

"My Grampa had a hog once that ate a clay pigeon and died . . ."

She was standing at the range now and she could feel his eyes combing her backside like the twin tines of a pitchfork. As he gazed on her, Lanie seemed to be gazing in on herself through the kitchen window. She saw someone taller, broader in the hips than she expected. She moved those hips slightly to see if they were truly hers.

Cyril said: "Say, could you give me a feel, Lanie? Just a little feel?"

She made as if she hadn't heard him. She put the bread in the toaster and thought about Aunty Pru in Baptist Heaven, resting in an immersion tub . . .

"Haven't had a good feel in a real long time."

. . . the bones miraculously restored to the old woman's broken glassware body.

"I had my sights set on you ever since you begun to round out some."

Yet it wasn't his sights, rather his hands, both of them, that were set on her now. Bear paws began to knead the firmament of her chest.

She turned and spat in his face, saying: "You aren't worth two cents and a fishhook, Cyril Morse. You can just go on home now. Or go see Rose Gagnon. Maybe she'll give you what you want."

And then all of a sudden there issued from his nose a flow of blood.

"Did *I* do that?" Lanie asked, all eyes.

Cyril wiped his nose with his sleeve. "You didn't do nothing, girl," he said softly. "It just happens. Once, twice a month. Comes on like a river. Christly nosebleeds . . ."

Who could not forgive her for being just a little disappointed that it wasn't because of her? She offered him a dishrag anyway. He took it from her and daubed his nose with it.

Lanie said: "I never met anyone that could have nosebleeds all on their own."

His face dressed down to a little boy's. "They say I must have gotten it from my other folks . . ."

"You mean it ain't entirely your own doing?"

"Don't stare at me so, girl. It's a curse. A real curse. Last August I bled into one of our hives and made all the bees swarm. And my daddy, he says I gave the little pigs scours because I bled into their porridge. He whupped me till I couldn't hardly walk."

Cyril Morse now raised his shirt and showed her where he'd been whupped. A scar arched across his flank like a rainbow. Lanie whistled. Whatever Mr. Morse used on Cyril, it brought out all the colors in his skin.

"Here," he said, rolling up a sleeve, "*that's* from letting some of the farrow into the tarweed . . ."

She touched the ridge of the welt that lay athwart his wrist. He was beginning to remind her of a tattoo artist she'd once seen in the State Fair, decorated from head to toe with strange animals and naked ladies. The man was prettier by far than the prettiest painting. And well worth twenty-five cents.

Cyril: "My daddy don't know when to stop when he gets that cowhide in his hand."

"I bet he wouldn't beat you so much," she said, "except you're adopted. He don't think of you as True Blue."

This telling him he wasn't True Blue, it must have driven him over the side. Because he was turning on the Niagara now.

"Don't cry," she said. "Think of something nice. Like shooting rats."

"Geez but I wish I was dead sometimes . . ."

"If you keep on with those tears, I'm gonna start in, too."

"I've been bleeding like this since I was a little kid. Always happens when I least want it."

"I know," she said.

He'd used up the dishrag, so Lanie reached him another. He took it, and took her along with it. Her wrists, then her waist. Placed his face quietly against her chest. Around his head went her hands.

"Maybe you're a bleeder," she suggested.

"I ain't nothing . . ."

She tried to coax his hair back into place. So it wouldn't stick into her like a bristle brush. So she wouldn't start crying herself.

His eyes sought her out. "Once, in church, my nose bled on the hymnbook. They said I shamed the Lord Almighty . . ."

Lanie rocked his head with the barest of movements. *Poor man! Poor boy!* Life ruined in a cascade of blood.

"Never could put it under control . . ."

"That's okay," she said, "I don't mind it at all."

"I tried everything. Lint. Cobwebs. Lying down on the floor. It just stops when it wants to . . ."

She was stroking his face with a finger that was a pointer on a map, moving into new country. Then all at once she heard Papa's pickup lurch across the gravel in the barnyard. It pulled up just beside the house. She could hear the doors spread open together like rusty wings.

Cyril Morse jerked his head away. He retreated to his chair and Lanie hastily returned to the range. Her folks arrived in the kitchen with a gush of cold air from outside. They seemed worn to a frazzle and paid Cyril very little heed except Papa said: "Always good to have another soldier minding the fort."

"We thought you'd be asleep," Lanie's mother said.

"I was, but Cyril came and wanted to shoot some rats with Frankie . . ."

"Well," Papa said, "your old Aunt Prudence lingered on and on and on . . ."

"She hardly seemed to be in any pain at all," Mama said.

". . . talked about the old times and the cold weather and Mrs. Casey from York that had kidney stones." His voice became a shrill birdcall. "*Mercy! A kidney stone ain't anything to scoff at.* How the old girl could even speak, I'll never know."

Mama: "She asked after you, dear . . ."

"Me?" Lanie said.

"That's right. She was worried that you'd taken sick or something. Told us she'd come and pay you a visit here."

The poor dear, thought Lanie, her face knitted to a frown.

"Oh, she was just ramblin'," Papa said.

"Can you imagine?" Mama said. "Broken back and all . . ."

"So you didn't miss anything, kid," Frankie said. "Just be glad you stayed at home."

And Lanie was glad, glad in her bones and all her flesh that she had stayed home.

Midnight at the Dump

Hazen Blanchard cursed and spat and cursed some more. He damned to heartfelt perdition the entire female species, including his heifers. For his wife Dorothy had just shackled off twelve years of marriage and thrown in her lot with a schoolteacher from Ellsworth. "At least Robert has brains," she told him. "You got nothing but silage and a little mulch." "Well," he replied, "maybe in life brains don't matter. What matters is, hell, I don't know. The weather, maybe . . ." "Christ, Hazen. You never even made it through the seventh grade. Robert is an *eighth* grade teacher . . ."

He was ripping apart her lingerie when Jake Partlow the manure-broker dropped by to offer his condolences. "Same thing's happenin' to all the farmers," Jake observed. "Why, Charlie Skeele over in Harrington, his wife up and run off with a computer technician. Can you imagine that? A computer technician!"

"What's a computer technician?" said Hazen.

"Hard to say. Guess it's something like a TV repairman."

"Women nowadays, they must truly hate the soil . . ."

After he finished with the lingerie, Hazen started in on the rest of her wardrobe. He shredded her blouses and dresses. He took a chainsaw to her shoes. Then he broke the crockery and savaged her bicycle. Now the only relic of his bunged-up marriage was a tottering, flatulent old coonhound, name of Scalawag. Scalawag had come as dowry from Dorothy's mother (her father was known but to God). And from the very outset, he'd been a wholly worthless tub of goods, terrified of deer, rabbits, even the common housefly. All he ever did was loiter mournfully around the cowsheds, looking as if he half-expected to get the hammer himself. Dorothy thought he was cute.

"Say your prayers, sucker," Hazen said. He leveled his shotgun and aimed at the wrinkly mass of ears, eyes, and muzzle that was Scalawag's head. The dog grinned an insipid doggy grin and farted. Hazen put down his gun. He couldn't manage it. Couldn't kill a fellow creature in cold blood. Hazen Blanchard was not that kind of person.

In warm blood was another matter. He bundled up Scalawag in a gunnysack and drove him off to the dump along with Dorothy's mangled wardrobe. Best place for all her appurtenances, the dump was.

Jubal Way greeted him at the gate with typical dump-keeper jollity. "Lovely day, ain't it, mate? Heard your wife left you."

"All of us got to eat chagrin sooner or later, Jubal."

He flung Scalawag onto a heap of debris. The dog let out nary a whine or a whimper. That's a good boy. Chin-up in the jaws of death. Catch you on Judgment Day, ole pal.

As Hazen was driving off, he was accosted by the dump-keeper and asked if he was in need of scriptural instruction.

"Sorry, friend. I got cows that want milking."

"Cost you only two bits . . ."

"Some other time, maybe. I don't want those teats explodin' on me."

Now Jubal Way was a man with a mission. And that mission was to keep himself from starving to death on his overly polite salary at the dump. He'd give scriptural instruction, hawk dirty pictures, purvey antiques, anything to touch coin. Broken marriages, especially, delighted him. He could offer scriptural instruction to the bereaved and at the same time plunder their throwaways. Never know when the refuse of a marriage mightn't turn up a vinaigrette snuffbox, a rubber-faced doll, or an old chamber pot.

But the refuse of Hazen's marriage was dismal. All Jubal could locate of Hazen and Dorothy's life together was rags and tatters and a gunnysack with a coonhound in it. The coonhound farted. Pretty unhappy marriage, Jubal surmised. But he took Scalawag back, fattened him up on dump slumgullion, and dealt him to a foreigner from Massachusetts as a champion soft-mouther of partridge.

Several days later Judge Parkin came by the dump to drop off some old copies of *Corpus Juris Secundum*. Jubal was still tweaking the feather in his cap about the gullibility of the foreigner.

"Dog? In a gunnysack? *Whose?*" exclaimed the Judge.

"Hazen Blanchard's. Guess he didn't want to be reminded of his wife."

"I'll see to it that he hangs!"

After forty years on the bench, during which time every practisable human folly had come his way, the Judge had a soft spot in his heart for animals. He preferred pigs to people, heifers to women, and puppy dogs to children. With respect to the fine points of the law, he considered homicidal maniacs a tolerable and even charming lot compared to farmers who abused their stock. Poor fellows would be lucky to be smoking Bull Durham through a rubber arse by the time the Judge got through with them. Same for kids who force-fed cherry bombs to mud turtles. So it came as no surprise when the Judge hauled Hazen before the bench.

"I was bluer than a whetstone, Your Honor. Didn't rightly know what I was doing. The old lady left me for a schoolteacher. You know how it is."

"I don't give two knobs about the old lady. Put yourself in the position of that poor dog. How do you think he felt? Imprisoned in a sack and cast off by those who purport to love him. Left in, of all places, the town dump. I mean, can you imagine the suffering of that unfortunate beast?"

"Well, I was gonna shoot him, but I didn't."

"You ought to be shot yourself, at the very least. But the Court will be lenient on you—this time—in light of the fact that the animal did find a decent home, albeit to an out-of-stater . . ."

"Well, thanks, Judge Parkin, Your Honor. Any time you want a deal on some turnips . . ."

"Not so fast, son. You're not quite scot-free. I asked you to put yourself in the position of that dog. Now I'm going to do it for you. As this Court is indeed lenient, I won't stick you in a gunnysack. But I do hereby sentence you to spend a day and a night in the town dump . . ."

"The dump??"

"Right. Perhaps a return to the scene of your crime will make you see the atrocity of your ways."

At that Judge Parkin banged his gavel twice and went back to reading the latest issue of *Reptile World*.

*   *   *

Hazen arranged for Ikey, his demented half-brother, to watch over the cattle. Then he packed in a flagon of back country

hootch, the likes of which six generations of Blanchards had distilled by the light of the silvery moon. His father had died hap-
pily of the stuff. His cousin Willy got hotter than a skunk on it
and had a vision of the Holy Family; Willy ended up a preacher.
As for Hazen, he figured that he owed himself one. Very little
opportunity for a good hard-core booze-up since Dorothy flew
the coop.

And so he returned to the scene of his crime. "Back with
more throw-aways?" inquired Jubal, his voice mingling hope
with chewing tobacco.

"Only throw-away is yours truly. Got a day and a night in the
dump for attempted manslaughter of a coonhound."

Jubal felt a little guilty about his part in this. Poor fellow had
only wanted to scrap a dog, not (as was the custom) a baby. But
Hazen offered him a swipe of hootch, which eased his guilt
mightily. 'Twas a damn sight better concoction than Old Trekking Boots; for such was the name Jubal had bestowed on his
own special blend of residues from discarded beer bottles,
Thunderbird, and stale rotgut.

The men passed the flagon back and forth and back again.
Hazen said he planned to take up self-abuse rather than get
married again. Jubal replied that spilling one's seed—on the
acidy ground, or wherever—was only natural in view of the cir-
cumstances. Were you ever married, mate? Hazen asked him.
Hell, no, answered Jubal, and added proudly that he hadn't
bedded down a woman in twenty-three years. There's fellas in
the Bible that went longer than that, said Hazen. Right, said
Jubal, I know of a patriarch from the banks of the Jordan who
went over five hundred years . . .

At length Hazen said: "What's the Good Book say about
eighth-grade teachers? They gonna enter the Lord's Kingdom
before us poor turdknockers?"

The dump-keeper picked up his Bible and checked the index.
He couldn't find any mention of eighth-grade teachers. Nor, for
that matter, turdknockers.

"Well, what about murderin' them? That ain't a sin, is it?"

"I'll tell you what I tell everyone that asks me about murder,"
Jubal replied. "The Bible says it's up to the individual. If you can
get away with it, fine and dandy. If not, it's better just to maim or
wound the guy. That way you got at least a fifty-fifty shot at your

rightful inheritance in the After Life. Of course, there's an awful lot of schoolteachers runnin' around right now. Maybe the herd should be culled a bit . . ."

A while later Jubal nodded off in the midst of a litany of murder-minded patriarchs. Whereupon Hazen was left alone with the night. A soft blue haze squatted on the distant hills. Twinkling stars were out. Also, an armada of rats was out—huge, potbellied animals prowling eagerly over mountains of garbage. One of them came right up to Hazen and regarded him with approval, as if to say, Well, one more rodent won't swamp the boat. Hazen yawned in its face. Yawned again. Pardon me, Mr. Rat, but it's time to catch some shut-eye. It was a few minutes before midnight. He took one last swipe at the hootch.

All of a sudden he heard a voice from out of the darkness calling his name.

"Who's there?" he said.

"Where have you been, Hazen? We've been waiting for you . . ."

"Is that you, Dorothy?"

No answer. He lurched to his feet. The voice seemed to come from behind some burning tires. He started to walk, in a stiff-legged, steady, drunk gait. And as he walked, he wondered whether his dear sweet wife mightn't be angling for a return engagement. Or maybe she was just after the farm, though Lord knows the farm wasn't worth a wroppin' round the little finger. Hell, she could have the farm and all its environs for the price of a one-way ticket to Portland.

Now the voice seemed to be coming from just about everywhere. Hazen tripped over prams, junked TVs, bedsprings, car parts, gnarled bits of metal, and heaps of *Reader's Digest Condensed Books*. At last he arrived at a sort of sinkhole where the burden of so much garbage had caved in the earth. "Rot my socks, woman," he shouted. "Show yourself . . ." And just then he lost his balance and tumbled head over shoulder, down, down into the sinkhole. He crashed through somebody's roof and landed SPLAT! on a hardwood floor. Now he looked up to find himself in a parlor with—quite spiffy for a dump—Home Sweet Home samplers and paintings of bug-eyed children on the wall. From across the room, Dorothy and Robert were staring at him.

"Well, you did say that he was a bit crude," Robert remarked.

"He's been drinking, I can tell," said Dorothy. Then, to Hazen: "You really try a person's patience. You know how long we've been waiting for you? Supper's been ready for, it seems like, *days.*"

"Damn if I knew you was living in the dump . . ."

"We were just about ready to call it quits for the evening."

"Christ, Dorothy. You run off and leave me, and now you say I'm late for supper . . ."

"And when you do decide to drop in, I think you could have used the door rather than the ceiling. Only yokels use the ceiling . . ."

"What was Napoleon's grandmother's maiden name?" asked Robert.

"Now, honey. You know he hasn't got but a seventh-grade education."

Said Hazen: "I thought you was living over in Ellsworth."

"We got a deal on this bungalow that was too good to pass up," said Robert. "By the way, when did South Dakota secede from the Union?"

"C'mon, honey. He wouldn't know that. He's only got compost in the upper story."

There was only so much a man could take. Hazen had a notion to rearrange a few of their ribs and perhaps break a stray collarbone in the process. But he decided against it because he was their guest and he'd always been told that it was impolite for a guest to beat up his hosts. So he just dug his fingers through the upholstery of his chair. Then Robert and Dorothy began Round Two:

"Look at that," Robert said. "He's digging a hole in your best chair with his dirty fingernails."

"What can I do?" sighed Dorothy. "It's the bad blood in his family. His brother Ikey is a genuine moron and he's got one cousin who's been in the State Farm and another who builds totem poles out of junked automobiles."

"Bradley's been out of the State Farm for two years," said Hazen.

"You do take the rag off the bush, Hazen. Why don't you tell us what he's doing now?"

"Twenty years in Thomaston for armed robbery," Hazen replied, not without a certain pride.

"Well," Dorothy said, "Robert's family are all highly successful educators and morticians . . ."

By and by she brought out supper and laid it on a tablecloth decorated with Robert's family coat of arms, the skull and crossbones. This, to Hazen, was not a good sign. It was an even less good sign when he took a bite from his Salisbury steak. He spat it out on his plate, which was also decorated with the skull and crossbones. "Damn," he said, "this meat's crawling with maggots."

Said Dorothy: "That's what you get for being so late, Hazen. The food's gone bad."

"I ain't eatin' maggots."

Dorothy pushed the plate back in front of him. "Oh yes you are. And wipe off your chin. It's covered with steak spew." She handed him a napkin likewise emblazoned with the skull and crossbones.

The maggots capped the climax. Hazen could tolerate things no longer. He flung his plate crashing through the window. Then with his handy little pocket lighter he set fire to the napkin, which fell onto the tablecloth, which also burst into flame, which spread to the curtains, which flared up almost immediately, being of cheap material.

"If I had known he was an arsonist," Robert said, "I would never have invited him for dinner."

Dorothy said that they would never invite him for dinner again.

Soon the entire room—especially the Home Sweet Home samplers—was writhing and dancing in flame. It spread through the bungalow quicker than greased lightning. Beams crashed to the floor. The floor crashed into the basement. Ladders of sparks fluttered up to the open heavens. All was fire and brimstone and billowing smoke. And even as the house itself collapsed, Dorothy and Robert were still complaining about Hazen's bad table manners in setting fire to his napkin.

*   *   *

Come morning, Hazen awoke with scarcely much worse

than a back country hangover. A quick check of his person revealed neither burns nor char marks. Nor did he see any sign of Robert or his dear departed wife, cremated or otherwise. In the bottom of his sinkhole, he saw only litter, litter, and more litter. The sun lit up the world and caused all throw-aways everywhere to glisten. Hazen realized he'd finished his sentence in the dump. He was a free man once again. So he brushed off his overalls and hopped in his pickup and headed back to the farm. He arrived there in the final flush of dawn. Now he gazed at the old silo leaning on its side, iron straps round its gut to keep the insides from spilling out. He gazed at the barn, nailsprung, unpainted, dilapidated, termite infested, and not worth the nether teat of a dead sow. And he thought: Damn place never looked nicer.

That very day Hazen Blanchard drove into town and bought himself a new dog.

Scenes from the Island

Four daughters. Four geezly daughters.

Each time Clew Ames bit yet one more bullet of misfortune. He'd inform the old lady she'd reached the absolute limit. No more girls. Then he'd launch his boat full throttle for Vinalhaven. He'd come back with everything sluiced out of him but his lust and he'd bed his wife like he'd been on a desert island for forty years instead of three days boozing it up on Vinalhaven.

Then came the fifth daughter. She had her old lady's charcoal eyes. She was the breaking point. When Madeline brought her back to the island from Rockland, Clew said: We're calling her Ralph . . .

Ralph's a boy's name, Clew.

Well, what about Perry? Ned Ripley had a mongrel bitch once, named it Perry. After that Arctic explorer.

But she's a girl. She should have a girl's name.

Clew gazed down at the little girl's face, which was red with tears. Looks like you been wakin' her in the morning with a lighted blowtorch, he observed. Whereupon his wife cooed sweetly to her in baby talk, a language they both seemed to understand.

*   *   *

Beers in hand, they were sitting, Clew and Ned Ripley, on the bare hummocky slope of Wooden Ball Island. The carcasses of twenty-five rabbits lay at their feet. Six weeks of stew. Thirty-three dollars worth of pelts.

Ned Ripley contemplated the carcasses. Wish I was a rabbit sometimes, he said. Just think of all that pussy, free pussy, no strings attached, goin' from burrow to burrow, geez . . .

Ned looked like he really did wish he was a rabbit. I got to hand it to you, Clew told him. Havin' no woman to cook your meals and such-like. I'd go crazy. I'm crazy enough as it is with Maddie. Hell, Nedsie, you ain't some kind of queer, are you?

No more queer than you, hairball . . . And he landed a hard fist playfully on Clew's shoulder.

Well, I guess there just aren't many eligible women on the island . . .

Only eligible women on the island are six feet under . . .

Ned's voice was a fist itself, half clenched. His eyes settled on a skerry just below where they were sitting. A cormorant stood drying its wings there. Ned raised his rifle and BAMM! the bird exploded like a kernel of dynamite had gone off inside it. The remnant husk was blown thirty feet out to sea. Clew roared with laughter. He saw the piss of youth in Ned Ripley.

*   *   *

The whole island seemed to be graced with sons. Chaney Perkins. Wayland Ames. Archie Perkins. Asa Young. To Clew there was no sweeter sight in all creation than Asa's boy Chris tinkering with one of Asa's junkers on a summery Saturday afternoon and the sky all bright and blue, the lilacs in bloom.

Rachel?

Nope.

Marylou?

No deal.

Clew, it's a mother's right to name her child.

. . . and a dad's right to chuck the name out.

But it's been a week and we still got no name for her.

Zeke's a good old-fashioned Down East name . . .

I'm not calling any daughter of mine Zeke! The baby in her arms gave Madeline authority. Clew backed off and headed next door to Asa's. Junkers littered the yard like they were Asa's notion of landscaping. And Clew would have gladly sat Madeline in the front seat of one of them, with Chrissie messing at the transmission, yes, sit her there in sickness and in health, through rain, sleet, and snow, for nine months or more, if it'd work some sort of sympathetic magic on her cross-grained womb.

*   *   *

The air carried the scent of hot grease coughed up by the pistons of Roger Halliwell's mail boat. It was the first tourist run of the season. Ned Ripley peered down at the deck like he was on a search-and-destroy mission. Will you look at the rising beauties on that one! he said in an awestruck voice.

Woman must be sixty years old, Clew replied, readying the crane.

Man, I'd like to grow tits like that by the acre so's I could run through them barefoot.

You're cagey as hell, pal. Ought to keep a watch on you or you'll be mounting the rear end of the mail boat.

Wouldn't mount anything with a propeller. Too dangerous. But I know a nice little dinghy on the mainland . . .

Clew slapped his friend on the shoulder. Ned hit him right back again. And they took turns at the crane, winching up crate after heavy crate from the hold of the boat.

*   *   *

The summer preacher was a man named Ammons who had heart palpitations and a wife named Amanda who seemed to own no chin. Soon they were luring everyone to the rectory with offers of tea and cookies. Madeline went, but not Clew. He said he was never much for talking with chinless women. A few days later, he was down by his shed plying whiskey bottles into toggle buoys. The preacher wandered down and regarded him silently. At last he said: What's that you're making?

Toggle buoys. To keep the warp from tangling around the trap.

I see . . .

It was plain the man didn't see. Clew went on: An' this here's rot-resistant nylon. Best money can buy. Synthetic.

You're Clew Ames, aren't you? I hear you have a new addition to your family. Has she been presented in church yet?

She ain't got a name yet.

Well, don't you think you should give her a name? So she can be presented in church.

Mr. Ammons, Clew said. You got any kids?

No, but . . .

Well, I got five of them. An' rearin' them up is a piece of cake compared to finding the right names for them. A name's something you can't undo. Man I know on Isleboro, his parents gave him the name of Cowplop. Cowplop Foley. How'd you like someone to call you Cowplop, Mr. Ammons?

The preacher coughed. He said his wife was expecting him. Something about a casserole.

* * *

Clew Ames, you're a brute! I wouldn't spit on your ass if your guts was on fire! What do you mean, putting that ad in the newspaper?

We're not rich, Maddie. We got to be Yankee traders if we want to survive.

But offering to trade your own little daughter for a two-way radio? Your own flesh and blood??

Flesh and blood can't call the coast guard . . .

Clew thought he saw the makings of a smile on the old girl's face. He didn't know anyone with a finer smile than Maddie, unless it was his late lice-ridden coonhound, name of Henry.

* * *

Clew: I ain't seen you layin' in any wood yet. You'll be cold as a fish this winter if you don't get your ass in harness . . .

Ned: I'm hauling myself to Rockland this winter, pal. No sense stayin' around this place. Nothing for me here, geez. My pecker's snarling at me something awful in the mornings. A man's tool needs oil ever so often or it'll turn on him like a wild animal.

Clew: I'm gonna miss the shit out of you, Nedsie. Christ, it'll be pretty lonesome here without you . . .

Ned: Blow on over to Rockland sometime. We'll light up the town.

Clew: Okay, if I can get away from Maddie and the kids . . .

Ned: Say, you ever name that little girl of yours yet?

Clew: Yeah. Denise. We was callin' her *the baby* for five whole months, almost like *the baby* was her name. Easy as pie to switch it . . . You'll be back in the spring, won't you, Nedsie?

Ned: Don't know. Depends.

* * *

Hard day. Northwest gales. Skies black as a wolf's mouth. Whelks ate the bait. Stick froze in reverse. Hard bitchy life. Hauling traps. Baiting spudge irons. Hard for a man in a cold boat alone.

Clew dragged himself through the house like he was in pain. You look like death warmed over, Madeline informed him. He flipped her the bird. Flipped it feebly.

Daddy, will you tell me a bedtime story? Kathleen, his eldest, stared up at him with big round childhood eyes.

Not tonight, honey. I'm dead tired.

But I'm not tired. I wanna hear a bedtime story . . . The girl hunched down in her bed and kicked her feet impatiently.

Okay, but it's gonna be real short. I'll tell you about the time me and Ned Ripley burned down Seal Island.

You told me this story before.

Well, first thing you got to know is Seal Island was a bombing range during the war. You know what a bombing range is?

But you already told me this story . . .

Well, the army raked over the place with all sorts of crap. Bombs, guided missiles, the works. Put land mines in every nook and cranny. Well, me an' Neddie boy, we got drunk one night an' so we blow on over there . . .

Later Madeline came into the room and found Clew with Kathleen, sleeping right beside her like they were two kids sharing the same bed. She shrugged and then put out the light and went back to attend Denise, who was crying for milk.

The Great Snake Massacre

The Eaton Brothers Traveling Carnival had a girlie show that rendered the entire male population of Center Wrexham helpless with admiration. The queue stretched down the midway, wrapped around the Human Pincushion and the two-headed calf, and passed the bingo booth on the way back. There were girls of every size, shape, and creed. There were girls for every color of the rainbow (including an albino Hottentot named Jezebel). At such a spectacle, even the toughest loggers found themselves muttering sweet nothings. It was the nicest thing to hit town since bottled beer.

But trouble was brewing in paradise. Bradley Kincaid, age sixteen, wanted to feast his eyes on Jezebel. The barker told him that he was still wet behind the ears. Bradley said he'd settle for Marie France. The barker told him to come back as soon as he'd begun to sprout whiskers. Then he pushed the boy out of the way.

"Well sir," Bradley said. "You just take it and stick it where the sun don't shine."

And late that night the boy crept back to the Carnival. He went over to where the wild animals were kept and opened the door to the cobra cage. "You just go out and have a rip-snortin' night on the town," he said. And the big snake slithered out and vanished into the darkness. Whereupon young Bradley headed home to study for his Civics exam.

The following morning Chief McGuire received a call from the Widow Hurst about an enormous snake on her front lawn. McGuire laughed his superior cop's laugh.

"It's true, Chief. I wouldn't lie to you."

"The Klan don't operate this far North, ma'am," McGuire said.

"I didn't say *stake*. I said *snake*. S-n-a-k-e. And I'll hold you personally responsible if it takes a chaw out of me."

"Probably just another hog-nosed bull snake," McGuire told her. The Widow saw tinkers in every woodpile and black men in

44

every shadow. To her, all commercial travelers were hell-bent more or less on carnage. Once, she'd rung up the police to inform them that the ghost of her late husband had invaded her boudoir for the purpose of extracting twenty years of nuptial favors in one night. But McGuire always put in a personal appearance whenever she called, for the Widow made the best fudge sludge in the county.

The old woman was standing there to meet him. She pointed with her cane at something long, black, and sinewy lying in a patch of her crabgrass. McGuire knew that it was not even remotely native to his beat. He emptied his revolver at the creature, which flared its hood and then glided off into the hedge that barricaded the Widow's property against trespassers.

"Goddamn dinosaurs," McGuire muttered.

"You just flummoxed half my garden," complained the Widow. In consequence, she gave him a piece of fudge that wouldn't have satisfied a termite, much less a two hundred and fifteen pound cop.

Back at the station, McGuire picked up his phone again. This time it was Ike Eaton. Someone had broken into the Carnival and let loose Candy. Who's Candy? asked McGuire, guessing that she was perhaps the strawberry blonde with the sequined bosom and the pert little bottom. Candy's my cobra, Ike said. Named her after that skinny Indian guy who went around in jockey shorts and got himself shot.

Now the truth dawned on McGuire. "Jesus Christ!" he exclaimed.

"Candy wouldn't harm a flea," Ike said. "Unless, of course, she gets a hair across her ass."

"And then what?"

"Oh, she'll bite and squeeze. That sort of thing."

"I'm telling my men to shoot to kill," McGuire said.

"Nah, don't do that, Chief. The S.P.C.A. would keelhaul you. Besides, I got a plan . . ."

And that afternoon a sound truck hired by the Center Wrexham Health Department roamed the streets playing snake charmer music such as Indian fakirs play with their flutes. McGuire had retrieved his deputies from Jezebel & Co. and now they stood by, armed with tarpaulins and seine nets. But day turned into night, the music droned on, the town came down with a bad case of tranquillity, and still no cobra.

"I can't understand it," Ike said. "That snake charmer music always works during her show."

"So much for culture," said McGuire.

"I'm telling you, Chief. My snake has the soul of a little girl . . ."

Jubal Ames happened to overhear this last remark of Ike's. He passed it on to his sister Myrtle, the official town gossip. Soon news was traveling like wildfire that the cobra had eaten a little girl, poor soul. Eaten her in one perfunctory gulp. Now the villainous Candy was sleeping off the little girl in some dank cellar. Now she was stalking Center Wrexham in search of yet more human prey. She was seen lurking near the Home for Little Wanderers. And lying in wait beside the Elementary School. And hanging from tree branches outside the derelict town library.

McGuire's phone rang at all hours. He did not have a moment's peace. The Reverend Mr. Ashley called up at midnight to deliver a sermon on Candy, whom he suspected of being Satan in an all-too-transparent disguise. McGuire took the phone off the hook. There came a vigorous knocking at his door. Ralph Shapely stood before him in an attitude of vileness. One of his pit terriers was missing. An undulating tell-tale track led from the pit to the piney woods.

"Ralph, that snake eats rats. Not terriers."

"But terriers eat rats, too. The snake might have decided to polish off the middle man so's it could get to the rats . . ."

"C'mon, Ralph. It's one-thirty in the morning."

"Ain't none of us safe, Chief . . ."

Ralph Shapely found his terrier in a neighbor's fox-trap, but that did not prevent him from organizing a vigilante group. Before long Center Wrexham was armed to the hilt. Townsfolk took to carrying shovels and pitchforks on the way to the convenience store or bank. Even the Widow Hurst got into the act. She began to hobble around with her late husband's Winchester and a purse full of dum-dum bullets. She said she hadn't had so much fun since news came over the wireless that Roosevelt was dead.

As for McGuire, he followed up every lead that came his way.

Usually he ended up in some forlorn pasture knee-deep in net-
tles and cowplop or drinking tea with a myopic preacher. Once
he stalked Candy for the better part of an hour, only to discover
that he was stalking an old rotten log. His deputies were beginning to show signs of rebellion. They wanted to get on with the
more serious business of voyeurism. And Ike Eaton had vowed
to sue him for assault if even so much as a single scale on
Candy's back came to grief. McGuire was just about at the end
of his tether when Miss Peters at the kindergarten rang up the
station one morning:

"I've located your snake, Chief. It's asleep in the cellar here.
What should I do?"

"Keep calm. Don't let it eat any of the kids. I'll be right there."

Deputies Mason, Cadwallader, and Pendleton reached for
their Smith & Wessons simultaneously.

Said McGuire: "Hold it, boys. We have to proceed with cau-
tion. There'll be little kids in that school. We can't afford to
bump any of them off. You know how quick on the legal draw
some of these parents can be . . ."

Then Policewoman Prentiss (née Sister Beatrice Immaculata
of the Little Sisters of Mercy) stepped forward. As a nun, she
had administered to lepers in the Congo, but had been forced to
return home owing to lack of work. "It was a terrible thing," she
declared, "but there were no lepers left."

"Well, what is it, Prentiss?"

"Just that we sure knew how to deal with cobras in the
Congo." A nasty grin broke out across her face. "Tear gas. We
smoked out the bastards."

"But we don't got any tear gas."

"I do," said Deputy Pendleton, who still possessed many of
his Vietnam playthings. He brought out a few exemplary can-
isters.

"They just might work," said McGuire.

"Sure you don't want some Agent Orange, too?" inquired
Pendleton.

Now the squad car took off for the kindergarten. McGuire
didn't turn on his strobe because he didn't want to attract attention. No telling what riotous behavior might result if townsfolk
caught sight of the snake. Nonetheless a big crowd followed
him as though they understood that this was going to be the

showdown. Most of them were brandishing hoes and spades. Several wore black armbands in memory of her whom the cobra had delivered so cruelly to Little Girl Heaven.

Miss Peters was standing with her charges in front of the school. None of them seemed bitten, squeezed to death, or otherwise molested by the snake. And McGuire wanted to keep it that way. "Okay, okay. Step back, everybody," he said.

"Can I have the trophy for my bedroom, Chief?" Fred Perkins asked.

"You're going to be the trophy unless you step back."

Deputies Mason, Cadwallader, and Pendleton positioned themselves by a crack in the foundation. Then McGuire tossed the tear gas through one of the cellar windows. The smoke rolled and expanded and filled the kindergarten. At last the cobra's bird-like head appeared at the crack exactly as planned. The crowd gasped. Now Candy came into full view, twelve feet long if she was an inch. Cadwallader threw a tarpaulin over her, but she slipped out from under it. Pendleton took aim and fired a rubber bullet, which struck Mason instead of the snake.

"Evil One, get thee behind me," said the Reverend Mr. Ashley, the Good Book in one hand and a scythe in the other.

"No, get thee behind *me*," said Father Murphy.

The snake seemed to look at both of them with the same degree of indifference. Suddenly her eyes, bright as polished jet, focused on McGuire. She unsheathed her tongue and spat a wad of venom which landed on his fly and stuck there like quicksilver. McGuire didn't know but that it might leak through and poison his organs of generation. He reached down and daubed at it with a Kleenex.

"Quick," shouted Pendleton, "the gook's getting away . . ." In his excitement, he hurled a tear gas canister into the crowd. Many of them ended up demobilized with burning eyes. The rest pursued the snake down Pleasant Street, up Market Street, across Central Street, and along Main Street. They screamed and offered each other encouragement and flailed about with their farm implements. The snake would hide under a parked car only to be flushed out again by a hoe or a scythe. Jubal Ames corralled her in front of the unemployment office and gave a thwack with his spade—but managed to thwack only his foot.

Candy slid into the Contasquam Savings Bank and slid directly out again, pausing only to hiss at one of the tellers.

Meanwhile McGuire hopped into the squad car with his deputies and turned on the siren. The loud siren squeal quickly deteriorated into a sound not unlike a dial tone. "Christly snake," he cursed. Policewoman Prentiss said things were never this mucked-up in the Congo. McGuire told her that America was something special. He swerved to avoid hitting a ten year old who was carrying a spear. They drove through town at a snail's pace for fear of making road kills right and left out of the local citizenry.

"Looks like our baby's goin' back to the Carnival," said Cadwallader.

"The criminal always returns to the scene of the crime," said Mason.

"You throw even one of them grenades, fella," McGuire told Pendleton, "and I'll see that you're booted off the force *instanter.*"

They pulled up at the somewhat barren Carnival. The line for Jezebel & Co. did not even extend as far as the Human Pincushion. It seemed that everyone had gone snake-hunting.

Now the heaving, murderous crowd arrived and scattered in all directions. Soon there were loud cries from the vicinity of the Fire Eater. At long last the good people of Center Wrexham had cornered the cobra. She was flush against the Fire Eater's ticket booth. There was no escape. She rose up and flared her hood, and then seemed to remain completely still, as though she knew that she was doomed. Pendleton leaped out of the car so he wouldn't miss any of the action. Hoes flashed, shovels and spades smacked, pitchforks rammed. Kitchen utensils stabbed.

Ike Eaton was shouting: "Don't kill her! Don't kill her!" But his voice became part of the general din. At last, turning to McGuire, he said: "They killed her. Just like they killed that skinny Indian guy. Just like they killed all those Kennedys. And just like they killed Marilyn Monroe . . ." In his voice was an infinity of sadness.

"Well," replied McGuire, "I don't think it's really the same as Marilyn Monroe."

Ike said he would never again play a town that didn't appreciate snakes. And the very next day the Eaton Brothers pulled up stakes and took their Carnival to parts unknown. Most people figured that he wouldn't have left but for the increasingly poor attendance at the girlie show. They could give a hairy banana about that. Good riddance to bad rubbish. We don't need any more filth in our town. Let the unsavory elements go back to where they came from. To hell with smut. And so on.

That same afternoon the Widow Hurst rang up McGuire with one of her triannual rape scares. He was driving out to visit her when he happened to see young Bradley Kincaid sitting in the gutter. The boy seemed to be in a blue funk. "What's the matter, kid?" said McGuire, leaning out the window of his squad car. The boy only shrugged.

O Lost World! O Lost Carnival World! Bradley Kincaid may have passed his Civics exam, but he couldn't care less now. For he'd lost his one and only chance to see the greatest wonder of all—namely, the Eaton Brothers' floor show, a paradise of nude women in all sizes and shapes, races and colors. From now on, there would be only death and prudery in a man's life.

Nightrangers

Pass the salt.

Standish quit chewing his food and gazed up. You ask for it right then, he said. And get your elbow off the dining table. Didn't no one teach you manners?

The boy turned to his mother. Could you reach me the salt? he said.

Challenged, Standish put down his knife and fork with a clatter. How'd you like it if I took that snowmachine of yours and set it in the barn? he said.

You can't. Engine won't start. You can't move it . . .

Oh no? Any more back talk out of you and I'll drag it to the barn with the jeep. Crate it up for the rest of the winter.

The boy howled. You can't do that! He can't do that, can he, ma?

Be quiet, Jamie, and eat your supper, said his mother. Your father's been up since five in the morning . . .

Wish you'd stop calling me his father, Standish told her.

Oh Clem. You're not going to start up with that again. Please don't . . .

His father died in the workhouse. Worst loafer in the whole Christly county. Couldn't even look after his own family . . . Standish's large reddish hand became a fist, coiled tight.

Meanwhile the boy Jamie had moved around to Standish's side of the table for the salt. Standish grabbed his wrist and held it, squeezed it. He would not have his supper violated.

You *ask* to get up, understand?

Standish had his reasons. Through the length of his years, he'd been taught never to take directly what he craved. Once as a kid he'd stolen off with his dad's underhammer percussion rifle without first getting permission. He came back home with three squirrels, and as he pridefully displayed them his old man snatched the gun and gave his hand a fierce drubbing with the stock. Even now the nerves in that hand would sometimes go dead on him.

51

He squeezed the boy's wrist harder.

Ow-w-w . . . you're hurting me . . .

Can't take it, eh? You learn proper manners, hear? Manners. Then something in him relented. He let the boy's arm fall and slugged him playfully in the gut. Left jab, right jab. What you gonna do about it, Sugar Ray? Jamie assumed a boxer's stance and pummeled his stepfather's chest with powderpuff fists, not daring to hurt him. He was grinning now himself. *Ple-e-eze*, he crooned.

Now that's the ticket. Standish picked up the shaker and handed it to him. He cuffed the boy's cheek lightly.

Thank you, said Jamie, taking the salt.

If you two don't stop fooling around, your food will get cold. And I'm not going to warm it up, either.

Hear that, fellow? When you're only a buck-ass private, best obey your sergeant. Else she'll put you on KP for a week.

Aye, aye, sir, Jamie said to his mother, saluting her.

Oh by the way, the boy's mother said. Jack and Nancy Granville are coming over later. They think George Griffin's been moving their boundary again . . .

Jesus Christ! Standish exclaimed. I'm not paid for 24 hours a day. I got to get some rest. You tell 'em I've gone to bed.

But I said you'd talk to them.

They can fight their own battles. I'm too worn out tonight.

Standish moved over to the stove and picked up a hickory log and hurled it in. The kitchen was not cold, but he'd been knee-deep in snow since early morning, slogging across half the county in what was, he felt, the dumbest search mission ever. He still felt snowed-up inside.

You phone those people and tell them to come over here tomorrow evening, he said. That's the earliest I can see them about a boundary dispute.

Well, I don't know . . . that woman sounded awfully upset . . .

Folks like that, they got too much money to be upset for long.

After his mother left to make the call, Jamie leaned forward at the table. He spoke in a charged-up whisper. I bet that old man was kidnaped, he said. He's in the trunk of some car somewhere. I bet the Mafia done it.

Standish chuckled. Don't get so enthusiastic, kid. Charlie

Summers ain't worth two cents and a fishhook to anyone. Crazy old geezer, no family, land, nothing. I'd have called off this search by now if I had my way . . .

You didn't have your way?

Hell, no. Concord thinks it's still too early to give up. Joe Ramsdell from the deputy sheriff's office is coming up tomorrow. We got to sift snowflakes till we find the old guy.

Maybe if it's kidnapers, they want Concord to pay, huh?

Concord's *already* paying. Search like this, it costs thousands of dollars. And for what? A guy who's just an old drunk. You ask me, I believe he just knew his time was up and he walked off in that blizzard happy as a lark. Heard an old fellow down Mousalake way did the same thing last year. Said good-bye to his family and climbed a mountain. Never heard from again.

They never, ever found him?

Disappeared without a trace.

Standish saw the boy was watching him, big inquisitive child's eyes burrowing into him. Jamie didn't want Charlie Summers strolling out to meet his Maker in a blizzard. He wanted action, excitement, spectacle. Scenes from TV and the movies.

Jamie, listen. What I do, it's not like the TV at all . . .

And as Jamie did listen, his head atilt like a puppy's, Standish felt a strange protective surge rise up inside. An incident from his own boyhood came back to him. Came back sharp and piercing, like a jab from a knife. He'd been about Jamie's age, maybe a year or two older. And he'd gotten it into his head that his father had to be the big man around town. So he told some school chums that his old man was a Texas Ranger who'd rounded up more bad guys than Wild Bill Hickok and Wyatt Earp put together. Oh yeah? the kids said, then why do we always see him driving a pulp truck? Standish had merely smiled as he told them that the pulp truck was his father's daytime job. Nights he became a Texas Ranger. Men like him were known as nightrangers, in fact. Stumpheads. Hadn't they heard of nightrangers before? For weeks on end he tied himself in knots furthering this lie. And then the kids saw his dad manning the town snowplow three nights running after three straight storms. They asked him about the ranger job. He told them they had been drinking too much ginger ale. Standish had been forced to hide out for the rest of that winter.

Really, he went on. This job's boring as all get-out. Tracking around after missing persons. Traffic tickets. Boundary disputes. Summonses. That TV puts ideas into your head that aren't always the right ones. You could get into trouble some time believing that stuff . . .

His wife came back into the room. No answer at the Granville's, she said. I'm afraid they might be on their way over here . . .

Christmas! They must think I'm their doctor. I got to be at their beck and call at all hours.

Please, Clem. They're new around here.

The phone rang and the woman, setting down her coffee, got up to answer it. If it's that Granville woman, Standish told her, tell her I've already turned in. A pain in the butt, these incomers, he said to the boy. Moments later his wife returned. She said, It's George Griffin . . .

George. Bet he wants me to do some conniving about that boundary . . .

No, it's about Charlie Summers. They found him.

Standish hurried to the phone. George Griffin's words forcibly pitched him into a geography that was not of the dinner table. The machine-gun phrases burst on his ear . . . Chase's deeryard . . . snowmachine upturned . . . lying in the snow . . . dogs had a go at him . . . better come right away . . .

Dead? Standish asked wearily.

Dead as mutton, was the answer.

His mind seemed to work without him. Call Ezra Steere over in Lyman, he said. He's acting coroner. Tell him how to get there. And then join me at the cul-de-sac with your snowmachine. The boy's machine's got an unhappy carburetor.

He slammed down the receiver and headed back into the kitchen. Those dogs . . . those goddamned dogs, he said to himself as he slipped on his boots. Those dogs were worse than any human lawbreaker. Mangling stock. Savaging deer. They put several days' work on his back every winter.

You're leaving now? his wife asked.

Sure am. Got to protect the site till Ezra Steere comes.

Can I go? Can I go, too? Jamie blurted out.

Standish was about to tell him to stay home and mind the fort. Keep his mom company. But he didn't. Different words, like they came from a different person, broke the hush left by the boy's anticipation. Yeah, he said, surprising himself. You can come along. Grab your boots. The ankle-padded ones. Double-time now.

He's too young, Clem, the woman protested. He's only ten years old . . .

Hell, let him be. It's only a dead man. Dead man can't do no harm . . .

But Clem . . . you know he just wants to do whatever you do . . .

You want him to grow up and be a homebody? He wants to go, so he can go. Might open his eyes some. C'mon, kid, we'll take the jeep.

YIPPEE!! Jamie put on his boots and hustled out like he had a wad of ginger stuck in him. Standish followed. Wait! his wife said. What'll I tell the Granvilles?

The Granvilles? Standish stood at the door. Tell 'em I went out to arrest George Griffin for jacking deer. Wouldn't be up at Chase's unless he was jacking deer. Inform them he'll get the firing squad. That'll satisfy them.

*   *   *

The jeep took the packed snow like it was hard asphalt. Houses and cars became blue blinking ghosts in Standish's strobe. He nearly sideswiped a Volkswagen that hadn't pulled over soon enough. That Morang woman shouldn't be allowed near a car, he said. The boy nodded. They passed out of town and drove five or six miles before they swiveled onto the old Brown & Dunn logging road. Jamie sat in his seat with a face of great importance. I never saw a dead man before, he said.

Same as a living one, replied Standish. Only he's dead.

Soon they left the logging road and joined a smaller tote road. Standish switched off his strobe. A waste of the battery in these untrafficked parts. The cost of a new battery would set them jabbering at town meeting about his "extrava-gance"—everyone's favorite swear word these days—and they'd reprimand him, make him feel small and worthless, like a little kid.

They were climbing steadily now. Branches reached out at eye level in the headlights. Plodding through crusty snow, the jeep drew up to where the road merged with a snowmachine trail. They waited inside. Standish lit a cigarette.

The last time he'd been up this way was a year ago in late February. A pack of dogs had turned the yard—Chase's deer-yard—into a battlefield of deer carnage. He'd been able to smell the gore a hundred feet from where the first doe lay with her belly caved in. Does, a buck, fawns—eight of them savaged, dead and dying, entrails straggling in the snow. God, how those dogs ripped and tore! They started with the genitals and ate up and around the flanks. Standish tried to get bounty money from the town so that hunters would be goaded into going after the dogs. No such luck. Too many of the dogs belonged to townspeople.

The skir of a snowmachine came from down the road. Some-one's comin', Jamie announced. A big Skee-Horse double-seater pulled to a halt in front of the jeep. For a brief second the rear end was lit up by its own taillight, and a bumper sticker pasted there leaped out in crimson 3-D: TOOT IF YOU LOVE GUNS. That'll be George, said Standish. Hey fellow, he shouted, You're doin' fifty in a five-mile zone . . .

Shucks. I thought it was a ten-mile zone, cop.

You made good time, you monkey. You call Ezra like I told you?

Yeah, an' I still didn't think you'd beat me here in that old buggy.

Wild horses couldn't have kept me away . . .

In his snowmachine outfit, George Griffin looked like a sack of raw, lumpy meal. He took off his goggles and swung his legs onto the road. Then he saw the boy and shot an accusing finger at him. He ain't comin', is he?

Sure. He'll help with the measurements.

Jeez, Clem. I wouldn't take him up there. That old guy's a Christly mess. Not something you'd want to show a kid. For sure.

Standish turned to Jamie. How about it, mate? You got a strong stomach?

The boy put on his most serious grown-up look for his step-father. A dead man can't do me no harm, he said.

True enough. That's true enough. Standish patted the boy's back. A real trooper, this boy . . .

In his eagerness to get on board the machine, Jamie stumbled
and Standish helped him up from the ground, hoisting him by
the armpits and plunking him down in the seat. Then he moved
in beside him. You got any extra flashlight batteries, George old
buddy? he said.

The man brought up a box from the floor and opened it to
reveal a half-dozen new batteries sitting on top of a pile of shotgun cartridges.

Standish whistled. Well, let's hit the trail. Sooner we get this
thing over with, the better.

A-men to that . . . George leaned forward and the snowmachine turned up the track, its headlights mingled with cold
moonlight. Jamie sat sandwiched between the two large men,
eyes straining ahead, tensed up and ready.

Standish's breath exploded whitely in the night air. Cupping
his gloves, he lit another cigarette. He felt himself go dull in the
sway and jostle of the snowmachine. Nancy Granville's ghost of
a face and slow-motion fish-lips lay in wait for him behind his
shut eyes. We came here to get away from it all, Mr. Standish.
The peace and quiet of the country. And this air! Don't you just
love the clean air up here, Mr. Standish . . .

That's dead bodies you smell, sweetheart . . .

His own body was starting a rhythm of fool movements.
Snowshoes on the prowl for the town drunk. Hands reached
down, again and again, to tap his shoes and free them up from
the heavy snow caught in the webbing. A friggin' Nor'easter
and damn if Charlie boy doesn't decide to take a little walk in it.
Mrs. Granville, too. Standish tried to imagine a scene where
Charlie Summers all stinking and drunk took the Granville
woman in his arms and made a kind of wino love to her in the
fresh snow.

George leaned left to make a sharp turn. Last chance hill, he
said. All out that's gettin' out . . .

The boy nudged his stepfather. You gettin' out, Sleepyhead?

George was nursing the throttle now. They bushwhacked off
the track, into a steep hemlock wood. Then they reached a clear-
ing of ledges. Standish's cigarette was a stub of ash, unsmoked
and drooping between his fingers. He regarded it with mild
surprise and then flicked it out. Can't believe the old coot was
up here in a blizzard, he said.

What? Can't hear you. The motor.

Standish bent closer and shouted. Damn foolhardy of Summers, hunting deer in a blizzard.

Before the blizzard, Clemsie. *Before* it. Then nobody will stumble on the blood. Smart, eh? You have to understand the criminal mind if you're gonna try and be a policeman.

Not so smart when the criminal dies in the attempt . . .

His escape vehicle was from before the Civil War. A modern model and he would have gotten away scot-free.

Better shut up, George, said Standish. You're giving away trade secrets to the wrong person.

Both men laughed and they were joined by the boy.

The next minute the moon appeared above the rock-faced crag of Black Jim just ahead of them. George braked and started to slew sideways, then gunned the engine and steered directly down. Halfway to the bottom, he gave his machine more throttle and turned off toward the right. Soon they were going up a new ridge. Get your flashlight ready, George said. We're close . . .

The sudden beam from Standish's flashlight exposed a rubble of boulders strewn alongside them like silent witnesses to their search.

Look! Jamie yelled. He pointed to a snowmachine lying on its side.

That's Charlie's, no doubt about it, said Standish.

They pulled up beside the other snowmachine. It seemed so entrenched there, it was like a part of the snow itself. George said: Those pre-'70 Arctic Cats ain't worth the price of scrap. And Christ, those skis! Warped worse than a couple of barrel staves.

The poor bastard somewhere near here?

Yeah. He's just about a hundred yards over there, beneath that little hummock.

Standish got out, followed by the boy. He saw that George hadn't budged. You stayin' here? he asked.

Damn right. I've seen this show before. I don't need to see a rerun. He reached down below the seat and brought up a beer and flipped open the top.

Standish headed in the direction that George had pointed.

Old George is chicken, he said to the boy. Scared of a little blood.

I'm not scared, Jamie declared.

That's the ticket . . .

Standish was moving quickly. The boy made great leaping strides in an effort to keep up with him. Wait for me! he called out. Standish's light zigzagged back and forth, strafing trees and rocks, till it came to a standstill on a figure twisted nearly double in the snow. Charlie Summers. The light lingered on him. Blown snow speckled his body.

The dogs had attacked the man like they attacked deer. His neck was a jelly of congealed brownish blood. Clothes pulled and shredded, like a covering of fur. Crotch and belly scooped out, eaten nearly to the bone. Then they worked backward to the man's butt, pulling him over and ripping off chunks of flesh as they went.

Standish hadn't seen a body this mangled in a long time. A body below the neck, that is. The man's face, though waxy with death and the cold, was intact and the eyes were frozen open.

A dog won't touch any part of the head, he said. He makes his kill at the neck, then lights out for the soft parts.

The boy looked like he was out of breath. He looked a little sick.

Go ahead, kid. Throw up if you want to. No one's lookin'. No one cares.

Jamie shook his head. I don't want to throw up, he answered, his voice quivering. He went on staring at the body as if someone was making him stare at it.

Pretty nasty sight, eh?

Yeah. But couldn't he . . . couldn't he just run away?

Couldn't hardly walk, let alone run. Look at that leg. Broken. Probably broke it when his machine overturned. He crawled around for a while, then the dogs must have caught his scent. Anything that's crippled, it doesn't have a Chinaman's chance in a place like this.

The beam from the flashlight grazed around in the snow.

Hey, there's his gun! Jamie exclaimed, reaching for the .308 rifle.

Don't touch that! shouted Standish. And he threw the boy a

bodyblock before he could get to the rifle. Jamie ended up sprawled on his back in the snow right next to the dead man. You can't touch *anything*, boy. The position's got to be marked, the gun checked for fingerprints. You never know what'll turn up as evidence . . .

And after he spoke, Standish knew that he had hit the boy harder than he intended. He didn't mean to flatten him like that. His light moved over the boy. You OK? he said.

But I thought the dogs . . . those dogs did it . . . Jamie rubbed his shoulder. He was crying now, a small boy's sobs, soft, almost measured sobs in the enormity of the night.

The Pickling of Rewt Chaney

Rewt Chaney stumbled into Loudon Falls one darksome day as white horses reared up in the harbor and hail pelted down and most townsfolk had taken refuge indoors, expecting the first Nor'easter of the season. Instead they got Rewt. A boozy midden of a man. Hair in grayish, dreadlock tangles. Ancient oystery breath. Garments that seemed welded to his person. That afternoon the weather cleared and the sky was awash with a brilliant blue.

Shortly afterwards people began to notice a strange smell in town. No doubt about it, the smell came from Rewt. It was a fearful thing to get downwind of the old man. Soap and water seemed to be his sworn enemies. It was rumored that he made a vow never to touch the stuff.

Along with the smell, people couldn't help but notice certain echoes of song in the air. For Rewt Chaney sang. His specialty was murder ballads and accounts of gore and bloody death. Factory disasters. Frozen little girls. Old-timey eviscerations. Double suicide pacts. Tramplings by cattle. Every once in a while, he'd slip in a piece about false-hearted love—and its oft-fatal aftermath. His voice was like the clapperclaw of deranged crows.

Around noontime Rewt would appear on the steps of the Great Northern Bank. He would just stand there and relate, say, the mournful tale of young Pearl Bryan and her sweetheart logger Joey Dale. Pearl's unfaithfulness would be brought to the attention of bank customers. Likewise a description of how Joey put a skeever in her and then chopped off her head with his trusty ax and left her body in the high count-ree . . .

Lem Prentiss, whose bank it was, thought Rewt might put people off their banking. So he'd hasten out and pass the ballad singer a dollar bill and tell him to be on his way. Then Rewt would head over to Pevelle's Dry Goods, with another song in his heart. A verse or two about, say, murdered lovers or back-country mutilations, that was all it'd take, and out would come Ralph Pevelle and thrust two bits into the old man's hand.

"Much obliged, Mr. Pevelle."

"You crazy old muck-a-muck! You come around here again and I'll wool lightning out of you!"

From Pevelle's it was but a short stroll to Cosmo's Diner. Nick Cosmoski did not exactly relish the man's presence. Sing away, you brute! he'd shout. And Rewt would. He'd run through a particular area of his repertoire and for an hour or so the town would hear about the world's great train wrecks. Passengers crippled by the carload. Fatherless infants. Whole populations crushed beneath boxcars. People in Loudon Falls would find their interest in dining gravely diminished. At last Nick would hand the old man his money. Tell him he was a damned nuisance and why didn't he settle somewhere else, like Australia.

By late afternoon, Rewt Chaney would have extorted enough money here and there to hit the liquor store. He'd empty his lone surviving pocket of its crumpled bills and loose change. "Three bottles of Thunderbird, if you please," he'd tell Art Morang. And maybe ask for a few bags of potato chips and some beef jerky as well (did all his shopping at the liquor store, Rewt did). Then he'd take his booty and head for his favorite shakedown under the railway bridge. He maintained that nothing was so soothing to a man's ears as a train rattling by overhead.

*   *   *

Loudon Falls was a decent place, and it tried to show Rewt some of its decency. Mrs. Andy Ames the undertaker's wife gave Rewt the run of her bathroom. In the forlorn hope that he might use a few of its resources on his person. He wouldn't. But cold nights he'd clump in from the out-of-doors and curl up in the empty bathtub and chug his rotgut. Sing loudly of famous maritime disasters. He'd wake up the whole family with the last wingéd thoughts of drowning sailors. As *The Lord of Baltimore* went down one night with all hands, Rewt was sent on his way. Afterwards Mrs. Ames told friends that the man was able to leave a ring around the bathtub without even taking a bath.

Next it was the Reverend Paul Ashley's turn. A man liable to causes. Picnics for shut-ins. Lobsterman's balls. Historical preservation. The Reverend thought Rewt himself was a kind of historical preservation. And that he needed buttressing same as any colonial saltbox. Tea with himself and Mrs. Ashley, he decided, would provide Rewt with that buttress. Expose the poor fellow to unknown civilities. Tea and cupcakes rather than cheap wine. Christian fellowship in the home.

But even Christian fellowship could not make tea with Rewt a success. The man entered the house listing badly to the starboard. His clothing was redolent of certain human waste functions.

"Sit down, Mr. Chaney. Please sit down," said Mrs. Ashley, so that in his discomfort—he looked like a foot stuck in the wrong shoe—the man would cease trailing filth across the floor. Rewt settled on a divan. His hand grasped a cupcake, which crumbled instantly to dust.

Silence prevailed. At first. Then Rewt leaned forward and said: "I have something I've been meaning to ask ye, Reverend . . ."

Mr. Ashley sensed religious inquiry in the air. When were the meek going to come into their so-called inheritance? Was there a special heaven for gun-dogs? Mrs. Ashley smiled. He was always able to turn such questions to God's advantage.

"Are you any relation to Jeb Ashley, the murderer?"

"Murderer??" The Reverend shook his head.

"Right. Tacked his wife under the rug down Jonesport way. She suffocated to death. They found her body six months later. Valuable Persian rug, I believe."

"I never heard about that."

"Well, the story was in the newspapers a few years back," Rewt remarked, and destroyed another cupcake.

"I don't doubt it, Mr. Chaney," Mrs. Ashley broke in. "Nowadays it's all violence and smut in the newspapers . . . if I had children, I'd keep the news away from them . . . why, it makes a person wonder whether or not we mightn't be savages at heart . . ."

She went on like this for some time. At last Rewt turned to the Reverend and said: "More mouth on that woman than ass on a goose."

The Ashleys never invited the ballad singer back. They said the man was a lost soul. Something that chose to glory in grime and dirt instead of the higher elevations. Mrs. Ashley told members of the Garden Club never to take Rewt into their homes. A week of scrubbing and spraying and ventilating and she still hadn't been able to get rid of the man's stench. There was something ungodly about it, she said.

At that point Lem Prentiss stepped in. He foreclosed on Bill Beal and drove Rewt out and installed him on the old Beal farmstead. Two dozen acres of acidy soil and lumpy hillocks, land so rocky that a person could walk from one end of it to the other and never touch ground. And Rewt was asked to farm it. Noblest trade of them all, Lem told him. Neighbors donated a ewe, a buck lamb, a dehorning iron, a rusty old push-tractor, fence posts, a caliper, and something large and metallic that no one could seem to identify.

"But my people were all ragmen and peddlers," Rewt protested as Albion Hammett handed him a scythe.

Two weeks passed. Lem Prentiss was on his way to visit the Widow Magoon on a matter pertaining to her late husband's estate. He saw clouds of black smoke billowing from off in the direction of the Beal place. Brush fire, he thought. It wasn't a brush fire, however. When he got there, the farmhouse was enveloped in thick flame. "Rewt!" he cried out. "*Rewt!*" Finally the old man sauntered out of the house, grinning as though he wasn't aware it was on fire. And he said: "Mornin', Mr. Prentiss. How're the kids doin' in school?"

The Beal farmhouse burned to the ground.

*   *   *

Then came the fateful day that Rewt ran afoul of Ike Cadwallader. Ike was eighty-five and a mass of varicose veins and he had some rare affliction that put him to sleep at the drop of a pin. He was blind in one eye and the eyelid to his other eye was propped up with a toothpick-like contraption. Occasionally this contraption would fall out. And then Ike would catch forty winks wherever he happened to be.

Ike was on his way to the blacksmith's to get his last molar pulled when that little pick popped out, *splink!* And his classic '38 DeSoto junker cleared the curb and rode up on the sidewalk and plowed into Rewt, who was busy serenading customers at Cosmo's with accounts of baby drownings. There was a dull splat. Rewt landed across the street in front of the cenotaph honoring the town's war dead. And Ike, he just snored away, the nose of his automobile lodged in Edge Boatwright's Blue Plate Special.

Somebody scooped up the ballad singer and carted him over to Doctor Dan's. The doctor taped and sewed and even (some say) did a bit of sawing. All the while pondering whether or not to accept Ralph Pevelle's bribe and let the old man die a natural Christian agonizing death. At last he put Rewt back together again. More or less. Whether he put him back together right is another matter. Townsfolk had their own opinions:

"You got the squirts, George. Doctor Dan's an honest, upright man . . ."

". . . and he screwed his head back sideways. And look at the guy's spine. Jesus Christ!"

"Go on. It was Ike's DeSoto done all that . . ."

"Only a *doctor* could do all that. Night of the accident, I saw half the town's leading citizens beating a path to Doctor Dan's door. Ralph Pevelle was there. Lem Prentiss. Albion Hammett. You think they went out of sympathy?"

For whatever the reason, Rewt Chaney was now but a shadow of his former intolerable self. He cast a pitiful sight hobbling around town. His head was always turned to the west even though the rest of him might be heading eastwards. But he'd post himself on the steps of Lem's bank at the usual time. And he'd let fly with the beginnings of one of his murder ballads. He'd get through a verse or two and then he'd stop in midsentence. Look to the ground like he expected to pick up what he'd forgotten down there. Then he'd just walk away, his head hanging a little, a sad and forlorn figure of a man.

One day Andy Ames was at work embalming Joe Morang the grocer's mother and Rewt shackled into his undertaking parlor. The man had an old duck sack with him and he emptied it on the slab beside Mrs. Morang's remains. A whole clatter of coins fell out, and some bills. "I saved this money up," Rewt explained, "an' now I want to be buried in style."

Andy was never one to refuse this sort of offer. He had figured Rewt for an unmarked pauper's grave. He was pleasantly surprised. "I'm sure that we can arrange something, Mr. Chaney," he said. "Yes, indeedy. We can give you a nice shady plot overlooking the Contasquam River . . ."

"I don't care about the plot or the view."

"Well, what about the coffin? I expect you'll be wanting something rather fancy . . ."

"I don't care about the coffin, either. Only I want to be pickled . . ."

"Pickled??"

"Yeah. Fill the coffin with the finest Jamaican rum you can get. That's all I want. Only make it the *finest*."

Right away Andy reconciled the strangeness of this request with the pile of money which lay in front of him. He said, "I'll see what I can do, Mr. Chaney."

Rewt must have sensed the end was near. It wasn't long after his visit to Andy's that he collapsed in front of the bank. He'd been trying to make it through one of his favorite mill disaster numbers. As a hundred people crashed to the ground with the dilapidated Sackville mill, Rewt crashed to the ground with them.

"See that, Jubal? A little early in the day for a booze-up, even for him . . ."

"Booze-up, hell. The man looks like he's . . . defunct . . ."

"Don't look much different than usual to me . . ."

But dead old Rewt was. People began to gather around him to make sure. Andy Ames had to fight a crowd to get at the man's crumpled body. A group of well-wishers accompanied the removal back to his parlor. They were in a somewhat festive mood. Andy nearly had to barricade the door to keep them out.

As per his instructions, the undertaker did no embalming. Just lifted Rewt's body up and installed it in a pinewood box. Into which he poured, one by one, forty-three bottles of rum.

That evening it happened that Andy was doing major reconnaissance work on Micah Hammett's son Jack, who'd been sucked into his father's combine, which had cut, threshed, and cleaned the boy thinking he was grain. Jack's raw gore lay in a kind of puddle on the slab. And Andy was none too keen on molding it back into a shape that bore at least a passing resemblance to Jack. The notion of drink kept nudging at his mind. But all he had were those forty-three empties. And the one full coffin. Andy decided that Rewt wouldn't mind. He pried open the coffin and took a drink from it with a soup ladle.

Now Andy Ames was not a boozy sort of undertaker. The job

of draining dead people of their blood did not give him a consequent craving for liquor. At this moment, however, he just couldn't get enough of the stuff. By midnight he was siphoning off Rewt's coffin into a fluid jar. From this jar he took long, gratifying drafts. Jack Hammett's mangled body didn't look so bad now. By and by it even started to look rather pretty. As he worked with it, Andy felt music brewing in his soul. He began to sing about a woman with a penknife who pierced her babes to the true tender heart . . .

True tender heart? Where in hell did *that* come from? He wasn't in the habit of singing verses he didn't know. Truth was, he didn't sing at all except in church and only then because Mrs. Ames kicked him if he didn't. It was most curious. He scratched his head. And sang away, his voice a caterwaul in the quiet night, about a frozen corpse named Charlotte.

Somehow Andy managed to haul his rum-laden body up the stairs. "Mrs. Ames!" he cried out, "Mrs. Ames, help me! I'm singing . . . I'm singing . . . *old ballads.*"

The woman gazed up at him. She wrinkled her nose in disgust. "Don't you climb into bed with me, Andy Ames," she said.

"I can't help it . . ."

"You can so. You can go and take a bath. You stink to high heaven . . ."

"But I just took a bath this evening," he said in a horror-stricken voice. And then he launched into one of his favorite train wreck numbers.

The Laying On of Hands

The first appearance of the Reverend Frank James at the pulpit of the Free Will Baptist Church in Agamenticus, Maine, raised every eyebrow in the house. The opening hymn was sung to a counterpoint of whispers. In the middle of the sermon, the subject of which was "Enter into the Kingdom," a plump Hattie Fawcett raised her hands skyward, shouted "No, no, no!," and dashed as best she could from the church. It was the first time she had ever seen a colored person that close up.

When the Reverend asked if anyone wanted to come forward, no one volunteered. The organist played "O Lamb of God, I Come to Thee" anyway. That hymn had always been the meat-and-potatoes of the service. The congregation sang it like they were taking part in a funeral.

Afterwards a concerned group of ladies gathered at Meredith Neddick's and they talked long into the afternoon. They had advertised for a minister, but they never expected to get a man like Frank James. A person would think that he'd know better than to set foot in, well, Agamenticus. The ladies wondered whether or not they mightn't be the victims of some awful practical joke.

"It's a mystery to me," said Meredith. "Anthea interviewed him and she wouldn't joke about a church matter. She had to have some reason for hiring him."

"She hasn't been herself lately," someone else said. "She missed the bean supper last week."

"And the potluck supper before that."

"That's not like her at all."

Anthea Peary's grandfather Ordney had founded the church because the local Congregationalists had not stood squarely enough on the Gospel. Ordney had been its first minister. His son Edgar was the second minister; and the mantle of Edgar's power, though not his vestments, had gone to his daughter Anthea when he died. The lay deacons all danced to her tune. She neither knew the Beatitudes nor the Prophets of Israel, but she ran the church with an iron hand. She appointed everyone from the minister right on down to the gardener. Only upon looking into a man's heart and seeing there the Holy Spirit would she turn him loose on the dandelions that covered the church green every spring.

Meredith decided that someone had to visit the old woman and find out why she had approved of a person so completely unfit for the job. The next day she and Faith Chase drove up the hill to the big yellow garrison house, the ancestral home of the Pearys since the Indian Massacre of 1693. It was a building both fortified and genteel, and badly in need of renovation. Twelve generations of the same family had lived and died there, farming the stony hillside for so long that they had become a little stony themselves. Anthea was the last of them, unmarried, the stoniest of them all. The self-sufficiency of the Pearys worked in her in mysterious ways. She was known never to throw out anything; the town joked that she even saved used toilet paper. All her old cars and her father's sat in the barn hopelessly bereft of life; they were washed and polished once every few months as if awaiting some miracle that would breathe life into them anew. For thirty years she had retained the services of the same housekeeper, Sarah Cardwell, even though she did most of the housework herself. She never did trust that woman.

Sarah Cardwell answered the door. She told Faith and Meredith that the old woman hadn't been feeling too well lately. Nothing serious? they asked. Oh just the usual, Sarah said. Arthritis, digestion, headaches, neuritis, her eyesight.

"Well, we must talk to her," Meredith said. "It concerns the church."

"In that case . . ." And they were led down a hallway that had a smell all its own, partly furniture polish, partly the fragrance of rose petals. Up the stairwell and into Anthea's bedroom, where they found the old woman seated by the window trying to clip her nails. She was still in her nightdress and she was wearing a nightcap out of which her white hair tumbled like it was about ready to take leave of her head en masse. She turned to greet them.

"Gloria, isn't it? Gloria Hastings. It's been donkey's years."

"No, dear. It's Meredith Neddick. Don't you recognize me? I'm here with Faith Chase."

"There! That settles it! I must surely be going blind. I've been wondering for weeks, but now I know."

"Blind, dear?"

"Yes, It's very curious. Somedays I can see the tower on top of Mount Aggie. Yesterday I could even see the hummingbirds at the feeder here. But most of the time the world's just downright fuzzy. Like I was looking at it through gauze." She offered them a great, full-faced, anguish-ridden pout.

"Well, I'm sorry, dear," Meredith said. "You certainly do have troubles enough of your own without us adding to them. But I'm afraid this matter needs your attention right away. You know that new minister you hired? I don't know whether you noticed it, but he's black as the ace of spades."

"Can't quite hear you, dear. What's that you said? About the ace of spades?"

"I said, 'You hired a colored person to be our new minister.' That's not like you, you know."

"No colored person had come through here since Mack Crenshaw found one picking over his garbage. And he was hustled right back to Portland. We won't have any riffraff around here, you know."

"I won't say this Reverend James picks through people's garbage, but you should have seen him in church yesterday. To hear 'How Firm a Foundation' on *those* lips . . ."

"Firm foundation, indeed," observed Faith.

"I hired a young man from Newfoundland. That's where he said he was from. He didn't say anything about being a colored person."

"But that's exactly what he is. A pickaninny pastor, that's what you hired. You should have paid closer attention."

"Closer attention??" the old woman sputtered. "How am I supposed to pay closer attention? I'm eighty-one years old and my eyes are sore and failing. Everything's just downright fuzzy. Why, I'll probably be blind as a bat before long and you'll still be telling me to pay closer attention. He told me he was from Newfoundland. That's all I know about the matter."

"I bet some of those Newfies are colored," Faith said.

"He never discussed his color with me. Mostly we just talked about my family. He wanted to know if I was connected to the Peary who went to the Pole. I told him those Pearys came from an island in Casco Bay. I told him we weren't connected at all. That was nearly all the conversation that passed between us."

"Well, I'd like to know what you propose to do now," Meredith said. "This man seems like he can preach a decent sermon. His Call to Worship isn't too bad. But of course . . . of course . . ."

The old incisive note crept back into Anthea's voice as she pounded the windowsill: "Enough of this. Bring the man to me!"

*   *   *

The Reverend Mr. James was chopping wood behind the Sunday school adjunct. His sleeves were rolled up and Meredith could see how thick his arms and wrists were, how enormous his hands. She approached him cautiously. She had heard stories, terrible stories, about colored men and blonde women, and even if her hair wasn't naturally blonde, it just might be natural enough to suit this man.

"Afternoon, Mr. James." She kept her distance, standing near the Sunday school building.

"Afternoon, ma'am. Pretty day, isn't it?"

"Going to make yourself a fire, Mr. James?"

"No, not at all." Seeing that she wanted to chat with him, he set down his ax and walked over to her. She stepped back. "I'm chopping this for the winter," he said. "Up where I come from, it's never too early to chop junks. That's what they call firewood in Newfoundland—*junk*. The old-timers would usually have it chopped and stacked two years in advance. Dries better that way. A lot of cold Arctic weather up north, ma'am."

"Winters in Maine aren't much fun, either." Yet it's highly unlikely you'll be around for the winter, she thought. She said, "Anthea Peary would like to see you again. She would like to see you now."

"Anthea Peary. Not sick, is she? She didn't seem any too well when I was there. Very frail, that old lady. But just as alert as can be."

"I don't think it's about her health that she wants to see you."

"She apologized to me about not being able to get to church. I told her to forget it. Anyone who's eighty years old serves the Lord just as well at home as in church."

"I think it's about . . . about . . ." Meredith could not bring herself to say it. ". . . your salary. Yes. That's what it is. I believe she wants to know if you'd be willing to take a slight cut in your pay. It'd be only temporary, of course."

The minister's smile vanished. "We'll just have to see about that," he said. "I've got a large family to support. Miss Peary must know that."

"I'm sure she does, Mr. James. She may be old, but she's just as alert as you or me."

*   *   *

"She's eating her lunch," Sarah Cardwell said. The visitors were brought into the kitchen, where Anthea sat hunched over a bowl of broth. She looked as if she was protecting the bowl from unseen enemies. Right away the old woman squinted up at the Reverend, but it was obvious that she could no more fathom the color of his skin now than she could before. Finally she pushed away her bowl and tried to fix him with her gaze. She said: "My eyesight isn't as good as it once was, Mr. James. I've asked you back here to find out if you took advantage of the fact. If you did, you'll get no sympathy from these quarters. None at all. Because, as I'm sure you'll agree, taking advantage of an old woman is highly unchristian. It is something I'd hardly expect of a heathen or a Jew, much less a Baptist preacher."

"Taking advantage of *you*? I really don't understand, Miss Peary. You stated a salary and that salary was suitable to me. Now if you've changed your mind, it would be you who's taking advantage of me, I think."

"Salary, shmalary," said Anthea with a flourish of her hand.

"My daughter needs braces. We need a car. I thought only Catholics bought that line about 'the beautiful poverty of the cloth.' You don't want a Catholic priest standing at your pulpit, do you, Miss Peary?"

"Certainly not. But the issue isn't salary, Mr. James."

"That what is the issue?"

"It is whether or not you falsified your, um, credentials to obtain this pulpit."

"My credentials are on the level. As I told you before, my

ordination came from the Nova Scotia Baptist Theological Seminary. You can write them . . ."

"I don't want to write them. I want . . ."

"Miss Peary wants to know if you tried to pull a fast one," Meredith interjected.

"A fast one? I don't understand."

"What I've been meaning to say, Mr. James, is this: Did you or did you not lie to me about your *heritage?*"

"It *is* the salary, isn't it? You really don't have the money, do you? And you brought me down here and now you expect me to work for nothing. Isn't that right?"

"No!" the old woman protested. "We have the money. We have plenty of money. We could pay ten preachers ten times over if we had to."

"Maybe you should tell him the truth, dear," Meredith said.

"Yes, the truth," said Anthea. "I am going to tell you the truth, Mr. James." She paused, then went on. "Mind you, we have nothing against you personally. You seem to be a very nice young man. But the cast of your skin, well—I have to be blunt—it's black. Which is not your fault, of course."

The Reverend Mr. James did not look in the slightest upset. On the contrary, he seemed relieved. "Ah yes," he said. "The cast of my skin . . ."

"You gave quite a shock to some of the older members of our congregation on Sunday. You have to understand that some of these people don't go out very much. They don't see much. They're what you might call a little squeamish." "The last colored person who came through here," Meredith said, "he was caught stealing people's garbage."

Mr. James presented Anthea with a smile that was almost genial. "I never lied to you, Miss Peary. I would have told you all about my skin color if you only asked me . . ."

"A person shouldn't have to ask . . ."

"Listen, I'm a preacher. I believe in the Word of the Bible, which says, 'Brother goeth to law with brother, and that before unbelievers.' That means I'm on your side, Miss Peary. We share the same faith. In a sense, my color is only skin deep . . ."

At that point Sarah Cardwell came in with a tray of gingerbread. "Tea, Reverend?"

Mr. James smiled. "Yes, please. With cream."

The woman removed the tea bags from the line where they had been hung up to dry, stuck with clothes pins. She put one in each cup and then poured the hot water.

"It's such a waste to throw away tea bags," Anthea exclaimed. "They dry out and you can use them over and over again. And now, let us pray: We thank thee, O Lord, for this bread which thou providest . . ."

Just then there was a clattering sound below them. The house seemed to shake for a moment. "Don't be alarmed," Anthea said. "It's not an earthquake. Foundation's settling, that's all."

But it wasn't all. Sarah Cardwell came rushing into the room and whispered something into Anthea's ear. The old woman frowned. She concluded the prayer: ". . . for Jesus' sake, Amen." Then she looked up and announced: "The facilities have just collapsed."

"Facilities?" said Mr. James.

"The privy, Reverend. This house is just so old, everything's downright fragile."

"It just up and fell right off the side of the house," Sarah Cardwell said.

"Next thing," said Anthea, "it'll be the very roof over our heads. And I'll have to pay somebody an arm and a leg to come out here and repair it."

They filed out, all of them, to inspect the damage. Anthea was helped along by Sarah. She arrived and tapped at the fallen boards, birdlike, with her cane. All that was left was the old two-seater and a stockpile of newspapers.

"That timber must be at least two hundred years old," Mr. James said. "Look there. It's rotted clear through. When a house settles, it makes mincemeat of wood like that."

"Well," said Anthea, "I'd hate to be sitting out here and exposed to all the prying eyes in the County. Do you number carpentry among your skills, Mr. James?"

"Built my own church in Rum Hollow, Newfoundland," he replied. "Built it with nothing but good timber and the sweat off my brow. I reckon I could restore your outhouse in a few hours. But then I really do have to get back. I have a sermon to prepare. Don't I have a sermon to prepare, Miss Peary?"

"You do, Mr. James."

The Reverend was allowed the run of the workshed. From inside the house, the ladies could hear him sawing away. They could hear him singing "The Old Rugged Cross" at the top of his voice. It seemed the most appropriate hymn for the occasion. He sang it over and over again, punctuating it with hammer blows. Sarah Cardwell, who delivered him a cup of tea, came back and said: "My, he has such big hands. I don't think I've ever seen such big hands on a person."

Anthea's eyes flashed brightly. She looked at Meredith. "I bet he could repair the church steeple, too. And at no extra cost to his salary . . ."

*   *   *

Nothing was achieved save the construction of the new privy. Meredith was furious. As she drive the Reverend back to the church, she parried the narrow road with an abandon unusual for her. She did not dare look at the man, who sat whistling in the seat beside her. Nor did she look at his hands, those huge hands which had been the instrument of her downfall.

Meredith thought: Anthea and Mr. James, the two of them deserved each other. They deserve to anoint each other now and forever with water from the same baptismal font. As for herself, that font was full of poison now. She would locate her faith elsewhere. She'd look into the Congregationalists. She always liked Mr. Ashley and his wife. Yes, the Congregationalists. They had suppers twice a month for which Mrs. Ashley made the best three-bean salad you could ever imagine.

The 545 Pound Boy

While the town of Loudon Falls was not exactly lacking in shack people, the Hasletts made all the other shackies seem like a D.A.R. sewing bee. God and their country they held in mutual low esteem. Schools they ignored. Likewise they had a passion for guns and weren't afraid to use them, knocking off a traffic light here, a Knights of Columbus sign there, as well as a more or less constant flow of family pets. Once Jake Haslett shot Ben Marlow's prize Afghan between the eyes. Said he'd mistaken it for a wood partridge.

Jake was the leader of the clan. Half the time he was hung over and the other half hotter than a skunk. Man hadn't worked a stitch since his youth at the broom handle factory. Work, he said, always constipated him. Jake's wife was Emmeline, a bulge of denim and calico rumored to be Jake's first cousin. More probably she was his second. Her idea of childrearing was to give the kids a bag of potato chips and boot them out the door. She didn't seem to care if Jake beat them up just so long as he gave them spiritual instruction in the use of firearms. How else would they survive?

And so it was that by the time they were twelve, the twins Doug and Don could jack a deer in a fashion that was pure artistry. Brother Ralphie jacked goats, sheep, and neighbor Howard Rathbone's llama (llama tasted not unlike venison). Sister Maybelle won the Rat Shoot at the dump three years running. Only Bobbie wasn't interested in guns. He weighed 545 pounds and looked it. All day, every day, he'd sit in front of the TV watching soap operas courtesy of an illegal hookup.

Last visit to town the Hasletts capped the climax. Jake puked up a sea of rotgut inside Parkin's Health Food Store where by chance he'd strayed. Emmeline and Maybelle cut a swath of shoplifting from one end of town to the other. Ralphie shot the Widow Magoon's cocker spaniel for supper. The twins borrowed the facade of the Contasquam Savings Bank for a bit of target practice; then they set upon the Reverend Mr. Ashley's daughter Tracy and threatened to dispatch her to Kingdom Come if she didn't take off her panties—which she was going to do anyway. Only Bobby would have no part of this rampage. He just sat in the back of the family pickup and ate chocolate bars and dreamed of love.

At the next town meeting the first, last, and only item on the agenda was getting rid of the Hasletts. Noel Ames, the selectman, suggested arson. That had worked to perfection with the Michauds, in case anyone remembered that forlorn family of loggers and purple house denizens. Right, Ben Marlow replied, but the Michauds could always go back to nether Quebec. Not since the Descent of Man had the Hasletts lived anywhere but in Haslett Hollow. Burn them out and they'd end up on the town poor rolls. Spreading their own special brand of havoc right here in our very midst.

At which point the Widow Magoon rose up and waved her cane: "I demand justice. Those bastards killed my dog. We're living in the twentieth century. We have ways of dealing with such people."

"Nuclear weapons?" someone inquired.

"No, the police. We'll requisition the State for a law enforcement officer or two. Hopefully a couple of those big hard-nosed ex-Marines. They'll come down here and put the fear of God in those Hasletts."

A murmur of disapproval wafted through the meeting. A call to the State would mean higher taxes. And that would be even more disreputable than the Hasletts.

At last a voice spoke up from the rear of the room: "Has anyone here ever thought of rehabilitating these people?"

All eyes looked to see the perpetrator of this remark. She was Valerie Honeycombe. She and her husband were foreigners from Massachusetts lately arrived in Loudon Falls to start up a Cheese & Yarn Shoppe. By profession Mrs. Honeycombe was a social worker who had switched to smelly cheeses only when she'd run out of back-country degenerates.

"You can't rightly rehabilitate what was never decent in the first place," observed Noel Ames.

"Everyone's decent, deep down, Mr. Ames," the woman said. "I have a university degree. I know. With the right sort of help, these Hasletts will lay down their weapons in a matter of weeks."

Said Howard Rathbone: "Fine words butter no parsnips, ma'am. You'd need someone willing to go out to Haslett Hollow. And none of us'll do it. Place makes the town dump look like (begging your pardon, Reverend) the parsonage."

"I'll go there myself," announced Mrs. Honeycombe.

The Widow Magoon crossed herself. Ben Marlow asked Mr. Honeycombe if his wife's life insurance policy was paid up. And somewhere deep within the abysms of the night a lone dog howled—then a gunshot rang out, followed by silence. Another family pet for the Haslett stewpot.

*   *   *

Next morning Mrs. Honeycombe got into her yellow turbo Saab and headed out to Haslett Hollow. The road was not much more than a pair of ruts, but she only needed to follow the primordial litter of beer cans and rusted-out auto parts and she knew she was on the right track. Finally she pulled up to a saltbox house circa 1790 that looked like it was being converted to a tarpaper shack. She was struck as with a flying brick by the odor of the cesspool.

Jake Haslett appeared on the front porch. He had matted hair and a face all squashed up like a road kill. "Tax collector?" he said. "Jehovah's Witness? Catholic Relief Fund? Girl Scout? We don't want any." He raised his .308 rifle menacingly.

But Mrs. Honeycombe knew better than to show fear in such situations. She opened a satchel and dumped its contents on the porch. Out came a veritable flood of beads, glassware, candles, screwdrivers, pocket knives, and a ripe Gorgonzola cheese. "For you and your family," she told Jake.

The man gazed down warily at the offering. He picked up the Gorgonzola cheese and sniffed at it like a dog. Soon a big glimmering grin appeared from out of the stubble of his beard. "Well, you're all right, lady. Come on in and meet the folks."

She was led into a room an inch deep in early colonial dust. The floor was several inches deep in potato chip bags and small pet bones. The dining room table was inlaid with grease. Mrs. Honeycombe sat down on a wooden chair because she didn't want anything crawling onto her from the upholstered one. As she sat down, she noticed the twins were aiming sawed-off shotguns at her.

"Manners, manners," Jake said. "Set down those guns, boys. Or at least stop aiming them at our guest. She's come here on a mission of mercy. Look at the presents she's brought us."

"How come you boys aren't in school?" Mrs. Honeycombe asked them.

"School? What's that?" one of the twins said.

Just then Emmeline came into the room. Instead of shaking hands, she gave Mrs. Honeycombe a whack on the back. "Welcome to Haslett Hollow, lady. Don't mind the guns. We just like to kill things."

"Ain't nothing more beautiful in all of nature than a gun," Jake added.

Mrs. Honeycombe saw her chance. "What about sunsets?" she asked. "Don't you think they're beautiful, too? Especially a nice red-and-purple sunset with clouds fading in the west . . ."

Jake spat. "Sunsets make me sick."

"Next time you come out here, lady," one of the twins said, "bring us one of them Springfield Armory SAR-48 rifles. Instead of these stupid gewgaws."

Emmeline smacked the boy across the snout. "Mind your manners, my bucko. These gewgaws come straight from the lady's heart."

"You oughtn't to hit that boy," Mrs. Honeycombe said.

"Why not? He enjoys it."

"If he enjoys it, you've taught him to be a masochist."

"He ain't no masochist. We're Episcopalians, but we ain't been to church in a while. Not since the Reverend Mr. Ashley spoke out against us from the pulpit."

"Just because we shot his angora goat," Jake said.

"Perhaps I could take you on a trip to the supermarket," said Mrs. Honeycombe, "so you might learn the alternatives to eating people's pets."

Jack spat again. "Supermarkets make me sick."

Said Emmeline: "Sounds like you're feeling peckish, lady. What do you say to some roast spaniel?"

Mrs. Honeycombe declined, graciously. She said she was a vegetarian.

"Well," said Jake, "I'm sure you won't pass up *this*." He

fetched down a bottle of colorless liquid and filled up a dixie cup for her. "Pure White Mountain hootch. Cures croup. Eases childbirth. Cures kids of spasms and worms. Not bad as a lineament, either."

Again Mrs. Honeycombe declined. Said she preferred Poland Spring water. With a dash of lemon.

"If you got worms," Jake told her, "this'll flush 'em right out."

She was getting nowhere fast. The Hasletts were wallowing in a Late Stone Age lifestyle and they did not even seem to mind it. They were worse by far than her former charges in Sullivan County who traded their baby for a secondhand snowmachine. But perhaps there was a ray of light with the other kids. She asked Emmeline their whereabouts.

"Well, Maybelle's out back skinning a cat. Ralphie's sleeping off a hangover, bless his soul. Bobby's watching TV in his room. *Hey, kids! Maybelle! Ralphie! Get your carcasses in here pronto!*" Mrs. Honeycombe winced. Emmeline Haslett's voice could smash a piece of crockery at fifty paces.

"You're the first one to show us any concern since Day One," said Jake.

"That's because I believe in people like you, Mr. Haslett. In a certain sense, you're the salt of the earth . . ."

Now Maybelle tromped into the room. She was a big rawboned girl about 6'2" who had the blood of a Siamese cat still on her hands. She took one look at Mrs. Honeycombe and said: "I think this lady's from the Welfare Department. I can see it in her eyes."

"Well, if she is, she's got it hid pretty well," said Emmeline. "She does a darned good imitation of a human being."

"Actually, I *am* a social worker. But I've come here on my own, to help you folks. Do you think the State really cares about you? Do you think they would go to the trouble of bringing you a cheese?"

"She's much prettier than the last one," said Ralphie, who was now standing at the door and rubbing the sleep from his eyes with a semiautomatic Luger.

"Last one?" said Mrs. Honeycombe.

"Yeah," answered Jake. "Welfare lady dropped in on us a couple of years back. Said we weren't supervising our kids. Then she said the State'd come here and cart them away if we didn't behave ourselves. The Mrs. wanted to kneecap her right then and there, but I said, 'Now, ma. Where's your manners? This woman's a guest in our home.' So we gave her a nice smoked terrier supper and a warning never to come back. And, you know, she ain't never come back."

"Well," said Mrs. Honeycombe, "the last thing in the world I'd want is to take any of your kids away from you. I think it would be just a shame. But I do think they should go to school, if only once in a while. Just to see what it's like."

All of a sudden there came from the other room a cry that sounded like a bull foghorn in heat.

"That'd be Bobby," said Jake. "I expect another one of those soap opera females bit the dust."

They picked their way into Bobby's room. Hunched there in bed, the boy looked like a dirigible in bib overalls. He was so enormous that his belly reached halfway to the ceiling and the bed sagged clear down to the floorboards under his weight. It took a while for Mrs. Honeycombe to determine which end was which. Finally she saw two little black beads embedded in a firmament of rosy flesh. She took these to be his eyes.

"Bobby weighs 545 pounds," Emmeline remarked proudly. "He's so fat, only place we can get him weighed is the scrap-iron scales at the dump."

The boy was crying and pointing at some sort of creature, bloody and half-skinned, that had crawled in through his window and was now standing however unsteadily on his bureau. It looked like it had just gotten off the boat from Hiroshima.

"Christly cat," said Maybelle, "thought I kilt that little bugger."

Ralphie drew out his Luger and blasted away. The cat collapsed with nary a whimper. All the Hasletts were laughing and slapping their knees except Bobby, whose face showed a certain alarm.

"Bobby's afeard of guns," guffawed one of the twins.

"Especially when they go off in his room," guffawed the other.

"Damn pervert, that boy," Jake said.

Emmeline gave her husband a whack on the head. "He's your son, daddy. Be decent to him. At least he's got a little skin on his bones. That's something in these lean times."

Mrs. Honeycombe walked over to Bobby. "Poor dear," she said. A flicker of interest appeared on the boy's face.

"I'm your friend, Bobby. My name is Valerie. I don't like guns going off in my room, either."

The boy's eyes, now limpid, settled on her. The woman bent closer, realizing at long last that she had a Haslett where she wanted it. "I'm here to help you, Bobby . . ."

His eyes, formerly limpid, now blazed with feeling.

"Surely there's something you want?"

"I want . . . you," he said.

"You want *me*?"

The boy spoke slowly, as if choosing his words with great care, dredging them up from his bodily depths. "I . . . love . . . you," he said.

Suddenly the room went dumb with silence. The only sound was the drip-drip-drip of cat's blood on the floor. The Hasletts looked back and forth between Bobby and the woman as if they could not believe their ears.

"You've touched our boy's heart, lady," said Jake.

"Sure have," Emmeline said. "Until you came, no female'd give him the time of day. They'd head for the hills. Disgusted, for some reason. You're different. He loves you, lady."

"I love you," Bobby repeated.

Emmeline went on. "The boy's nearly twenty years old. It's time he settled down, got himself a wife . . ."

Mrs. Honeycombe was beginning to feel that it would not be healthy for her to remain in Haslett Hollow much longer. She gazed at her watch rather obviously. "Oh dear," she said, "it's almost noon. I really must be getting back to my Cheese & Wine Shoppe . . ."

"You're his," Jake said, raising his .308, "and he's your'n . . ."

Last voice Mrs. Honeycombe heard before she fainted was Ralphie's, who said something about shooting a Great Dane to celebrate the marriage.

*   *   *

A couple of years later, a woman of indeterminate age straggled into the town of Loudon Falls. She was somewhat overweight and more than somewhat dirty and her hair was matted with grease and obscure food particles. This woman bore a passing resemblance to the bygone Mrs. Honeycombe who had vanished from the face of the earth one fine summer morning. But that Mrs. Honeycombe had been a person of some repute. This woman was a poor hapless thing, clearly demented. Over and over again all she could say was: "I was only his plaything, I was only his plaything . . ." The good citizens of Loudon Falls pitched together and gave her a one-way ticket to the State Farm.

As for the Hasletts, they came into town same as before, knocking off traffic lights, stop signs, and family pets. Emmeline and Maybelle continued to steal anything that wasn't chained down. Ralphie and the twins still used the Contasquam Savings Bank for target practice. And Bobby remained as usual sprawled out in the back of the ancient pickup (updated with turbo Saab parts). He still weighed 545 pounds and still looked like a dirigible in bib overalls. But now he was joined by a boy child fat as a butterball and twice as healthy who, according to one far-fetched local legend, was said to be his own son.

The Standing Stone

The South African girl came during a warm spell in late May, and Michael McDonough set her digging potatoes and turnips in his garden. He could thus fasten his eyes unchecked to her plump backside and the bulge of skin that peered out between her jeans and blouse. This skin was light and had freckles like midges, which Michael would have liked to press as though they were midges. But he didn't press them at all. Instead he chose to squat down next to the girl, the better to inform her of certain things. In a low conspiratorial voice, he'd lecture her on herbs, which she always seemed to mistake for weeds. Or he'd pelt her with gentle obscenities, his eyes doing a dance with her big violet eyes. "Shit and bread are brothers," he'd tell her. And she would giggle, "Crumbs, you are foul."

Their physical closeness, Michael figured, would not escape the predatory notice of his neighbors, most of whom were pensioners. He rather hoped that they'd think some sort of intimacy, some peculiar secret of the flesh, existed between himself and the girl. But there was nothing like that, nothing at all, between them. During her stay, he didn't touch her once.

"Well, I'm off," the girl announced at last. And she left him her home address, in Capetown. She also left him, who dwelt among the illiterate seasons, a small volume of Yeats's poems.

"Well, Michael. Who'll dig your spuds now?" inquired Patrick Doyle, the shopkeeper in Cahermore.

"There'll be a brigade of them coming from South Africa soon enough."

"You only need one, man."

"I'm planning on hiring out my spares," Michael said.

Patrick chose this moment, with Michael seemingly lost to a world of women, to deliver his lethal blow. "'Baccy's up to a pound, you know . . ."

"That's the limit. The bloody limit. I can't afford those prices and the ewes having a bad year of it and all."

Still, he emptied his pockets of loose change, whereupon he received his block of plug.

"I'm not blaming you, Patrick. But this country is coming to a bad end when a man can't even afford a bit of a smoke now and then."

Excluding the priest and the publican, Patrick Doyle was the only man in Cahermore not on the dole, a fact which often plunged him into welters of self-doubt. His moneymaking made him feel quite alone. Now, as he watched Michael walk away, he felt like a thief, and worse. For a thief steals from rich men and he had just taken money from a poor man. Or, if not a poor man, at least a hopeless one.

Later Patrick said to his wife: "A man like Michael McDonough, he's got ten more years before the pension. What's he to do until then? Prices keep going up and the dole only just stays the same."

"Let him go out and get a job. Do something. Emigrate. There's too many bachelors in this parish as it is."

"Michael's the right rogue with women. Always was."

"There. Let him get married then."

*   *   *

The road from the village to Michael's house was an uphill meandering that looped together half the houses in the parish before coming to an end in a bog. Usually Michael could take the hill with easy strides in twenty minutes. But today there was clay at his feet and a certain lethargy swamping his head. He stopped to slice off a few shavings from his bar of plug and rolled them between his palms. Then he scraped the dottle from the bottom of his pipe and mixed it with the new brown fibers. As he was stuffing this mixture into his bowl, his eye caught two figures approaching him on bicycles, their rucksacks emblazoned with the Stars and Stripes. Two more Americans, he thought.

He knew precisely where the Americans were headed: to examine his standing stone. The stone was not really his, it just happened to lie in the middle of his barley field. It was the property of the Division of Public Monuments, which dispatched an annual inspector to check it out. Such surveillance was necessary, one of these inspectors had told him, as long as people remained ignorant of their heritage. There had been a farmer in Kerry who had torn down a twelfth-century abbey, stone by stone, to construct a wall around his garden. "I've already a wall around my garden," Michael informed the inspector. "I didn't mean to accuse you personally, Mr. McDonough," the man told him, "but most country people today wouldn't give tuppence for that stone." Then he walked Michael over to the stone, to show him at first hand its antiquarian virtues. "You see these notches cut into the edge up there? That's Ogham script, and it dates from the seventh century A.D." "My father used to consult the stone concerning the whereabouts of his missing cattle," Michael remarked. "Quite so," said the inspector.

Sure enough, when he got home, Michael saw the two Americans in an attitude of intense scrutiny beside the stone. Pipe in mouth, he waited beside the garden wall. Finally, one of the Americans, a boy of about twenty, wandered over to him and with a nod and a wave of his guidebook said:

"Excuse me, but do you know anything about that old stone? My book doesn't say anything about it except 'Worth a visit if you happen to be in the area.'"

"Well, you're in the area, all right, and the stone is well worth the visit. It was put there by the Druids hundreds of years ago. One of their great leaders is buried there. If you stand next to it of a night, you can hear them keening for him."

"And have you ever heard them . . . keening?"

"I have. Many times." Michael marked his acquaintance with the supernatural casually, by knocking the ashes out of his pipe. He had told this same story to the South African girl when she first arrived at his door, her own guidebook in hand, inquiring about "an interesting example of a Celtic monolith." She said that she'd looked all around but just couldn't find the object in question. "Haven't you eyes in your head, woman?" he asked with mock gruffness, before leading her out to his barley field, where the stone stood unmistakably. Her expression indicated that she didn't find it "an interesting example" of anything. "Oh, I saw that," she said. "I didn't think it was the monolith, though." "It's the monolith, all right," Michael told her. "And if you put your ear to it at night, you can hear the very ancient people keening . . ."

The South African girl had never heard ancient people keening. She thought it might be rather exciting. Sipping cup after cup of tea, she sat with Michael into the night. She told him that she found Ireland a very nice country, despite the troubles in the North. The people had been generous to her, regaling her with food and digs, so nice of them not to charge her for things. "Don't you have any other word but 'nice'?" Michael prodded her and she responded with a great glimmering grin, because she knew in her heart that Michael was nice, too. She soon lost her curiosity about his stone. When she began to talk about spending the night in "some horrid abandoned shed," he created a makeshift bed for her on his kitchen floor. And the next day, when she began to complain about the high price of hotel rooms, he told her that she could stay as long as she liked, "only you'll have to be of some use around the house, woman."

With a little scrubbing, Michael's floor became more or less presentable. The South African girl decided to maintain her residence there. The worn flagstones were reasonably comfortable and more than reasonably quaint. Besides, she didn't want to tempt fate by proposing any other sleeping arrangement. Maybe one day Michael would demand a physical return on his generosity; if it came to that, the girl decided, she would pack her bags and move on. But it never did come to that. Michael seemed too dedicated to the respectable distance between them to want it violated.

*   *   *

The second American, lanky and towheaded, walked over to where his friend was chatting with Michael about the Druids. Around his neck dangled a camera, which he pressed to his chest with each loping stride. "Why don't you take this man's picture in front of that stone?" his friend suggested.

Michael was gestured over to the stone. He didn't know what to do with his pipe, whether to leave it in his mouth or bury it in his coat pocket. He was photographed carrying it en route from his mouth to his pocket. "The picture'll be a little blurry, that's all," the towheaded boy told him, and promised him a copy of the print.

"Would you lads care for a cup of tea?" Michael asked as they began to rearrange their gear, strap their effects to various parts of their bicycles.

"My name's Jim, and he, well, his name is Jim, too," said the first boy. He had never been referred to as a "lad" before, and the word at first took him by surprise, until he recognized its innate charm. He agreed, yes, a cup of tea would hit the spot. So the two of them followed Michael into his kitchen, which had begun to exhibit a certain untidiness in the days since the South African girl's departure.

"Did you say you were married?" the first Jim asked.

"I'm not, of course. What good is marriage to men like ourselves?" Michael chuckled.

"Your culture must not be too big on marriage."

"Culture? Who said anything about culture? I'm happy the way I am. Women are all a cod. I wouldn't marry one if her backside was studded with diamonds."

"I bet."

"I can see the heat of marriage is on yez both." He smiled. They smiled as well. Then the first Jim turned to the second Jim. "This man was telling me about that stone. He said it was placed there by the Druids and if you listen to it, you can hear them crying . . ."

"It's only in the middle of the night," Michael interrupted, "only then you can hear them. That's when they're in their prime. If you'd stay till midnight you could hear them for yourselves."

"We'd stay, but we have to be at the Allihies hostel by ten," the second Jim said.

As they drank their tea, Michael asked them did they want some bread and butter. They said they didn't want to be any trouble. He said no trouble at all, and sliced the wheaten loaf so quickly that he created a detritus of crumbs.

"Look, we're not really hungry at all."

Michael ignored this refusal, which he took to be a sign of good manners. He sliced at the loaf again. "There. Eat that." The two Americans stared at the mountain of bread at their disposal.

"They say it's all violence in American today, that you wouldn't want to step out at night for fear of being murdered on your own doorstep."

"Who said that?" the first Jim exclaimed. "Most of America is safer than Ireland. Take Indiana, for example. Where we're from. We've got no real crime there."

"Indiana, is it? You must have a good many Indians there."

"Very few, in fact. And the few we have are just like you and me. They drive around in expensive cars and everything."

"The Indians were once the finest light cavalry in the world," Michael asserted. It was such a treat to talk to traveled people. He wanted to hear more about Indiana. And he wanted to hear about the famous American darkies, to find out whether they were rotters, like the South African variety. Suddenly he felt quite small in his ignorance, cramped by his own yesterdays. Worse than a young heifer he was. Sentenced forever to this twisting of dung-filled roads and pocket fields, to the same dreary, purblind looks of his neighbors. Then he remembered that he had to bring the cows down from the mountain.

"If you lads will excuse me for a few minutes . . ."

"We should be going, anyway." They rose, smiles pasted across their faces. Michael noticed that a small corncob pipe had slipped out of the towheaded boy's pocket. It seemed like a child's toy. He picked it up and handed it to the boy, who was bending over to fasten his bicycle clips.

"Will you stay and have a bit of a smoke, then?" he inquired. He brought out his plug of tobacco and waved it teasingly in front of the American's face. The boy looked a little startled.

"That's tobacco?"

"By God, it is. The best in the world." By way of illustration, he kindled his pipe. The room was soon filled with a pungent odor much like burning heather. Michael placed the tobacco in the boy's hand. His own hand went to the boy's shoulder.

"We really have to go now," piped up the other American. And before Michael knew it, they were both at his door, extending their thanks, waving their good-byes. The clay was at his feet again. He couldn't stop their retreat into the dusk. He almost called out after them to ask if they wanted to take the bread with them. But he didn't.

"He's a very queer man," observed the first Jim once they had mounted their bicycles.

"He's a queer," his friend shot back. He could still feel the hand on his shoulder.

*   *   *

The next morning swords of rain slashed the knuckly hills. At first Michael thought someone was tossing pebbles against his window. "Bugger off," he shouted before he was fully awake. Then he saw a few erratic rivulets under his door. He stumbled to the window and groaned. He groaned again as his coldly wakeful brain now reminded him that he had a cow nearly ready to calve.

He thrust his pipe into his mouth and began to search around for his plug. Then he remembered the two Americans, with their itch for the road. They had made off with his last bit of tobacco.

The rain hadn't let up by the time he emerged from his house for the trek down to Patrick's. He felt its force against his oilskin like a mountain of loose silk. It quickly seeped through his shoes, his socks, his skin.

"Bad day, Michael," Patrick greeted him.

"Rotten. I'm wetter than an eel."

"The wireless says we'll be getting this weather on through the weekend. Bad for the tourist. Bad for everybody. What'll it be?"

"A bottle of Jeyes fluid. The old girl'll be calving any day now. Bad weather for mucking about with cattle, Patrick."

The white bottle Patrick placed on the counter gave Michael an unsettling image of all the calves his midwifery had brought forth. Wet with birth, they were arranged in his mind like churchgoers, row upon row of them. Their red, curly heads were lifted in dumb adoration: a look that expressed the whole of their lives. They were dumb in birth and dumb in death, and in between they grazed away dumbly at some stunted bit of pasturage.

"Get me a plug of tobacco while you're at it," he said, pocketing the bottle.

"You're out of luck there, Michael. A German came in and bought the last of it yesterday evening. 'Tis the tourist season, you know. You'll just have to wait till the lorry comes in from Castletown next week."

Michael adjourned to Sean Twoomey's across the road. "Fuckin' foreigners," he muttered to Sean. "It's the fuckin' foreigners who're buying up everything in this country now." He ordered a bottle of stout.

"Ah, they're not so bad, Michael," replied Sean. "You've got to realize that these people are bringing in the business. We all depend on business, so we do."

"I don't."

During the next hour, Michael lost his hold on sobriety. He switched to straight whiskeys, and when a Dutch holiday-maker and his wife sat down next to him, he asked them would they pay ten shillings apiece to come up and see his stone. Leaning closer, he told them that he shot at visitors who refused to pay. Both of them offered him tolerant smiles. Soon he was yelling over to Sean, "For God's sakes, man, give me another whiskey before these damned tourists drink it all up."

"You should be thinking of going home, Michael. You've too much drink on you as it is and you're creating a disturbance with the other patrons."

Michael rose to protest and he fell headlong across the table before slithering to the floor in a ruin of whiskey and stout and broken glass. The Dutchman took his arm. "Leave off your help," Michael said, jerking loose. "I'm my own master." And he nearly lost his balance again.

"You're in the horrors with drink," Sean exclaimed and hurried over with a brush to dust off Michael's coat. He stood him against the door like a heavy sack of grain. "You stay there now. Tom MacIntyre will be along any time now and he'll take you home in his car."

Michael didn't care to wait for Tom MacIntyre. The hard rain had now tapered off to a fleece of drizzle, so he set out on his own. Soon he was negotiating the revelry of the road. For every step he took forward, this road would dance him two or three steps to one side. Once it even dumped him in some low-set hedges, and briars scythed across his face before joining hands again.

When he was nearly home, he saw two people, a man and a woman, moving across his barley field. Holding hands, they were engrossed in conversation and did not appear to notice him. Their accents proclaimed them Dubliners. But what difference did that make? Dubliners, like everyone else, were a gruesome lot. Michael squinted over at his stone to determine whether any traces of its sanctity still remained. All he could see in the mist was the blur of a long forefinger, pointing skywards.

"Fuckin' tourists probably pissed on it. They use us like a public lavatory."

He jammed his pipe between his teeth and wondered if he could borrow tobacco from any of these blackguards. Perhaps Patrick's German friend might visit his barley field. He might be able to nail the man for a few pipefuls. Better yet, prevent anyone from ever trekking across his barley fields again. Let them kiss the bloody Blarney Stone till they're bloody blue in the face.

A rock-hard singleness of purpose now succeeded the liquor in Michael's veins. He went into the byre where he kept his tools and farming implements and where his big-bellied cow now turned and lowed at him through her nostrils, the chain round her neck rattling. Soon his eyes focused on an old chipping hammer covered with the bearded grayness of spiderwebs. During a work-sojourn in Cork city, he'd used this hammer to knock salt off the boilers of tramp steamers. But now it was too far gone. Right next to it, however, lay a sledgehammer that he had wielded just last year at the road-mending. Michael grasped it, throttled it, struck it against a rusted milk churn. The churn split in two.

Shrouded by the mist, the stone looked as vulnerable as mist itself. Michael advanced toward it discreetly, for he didn't want anyone to see him. Then he ran his hands up and down the rigid height. His entire body grew taut in challenge. He hit the stone a violent blow with his hammer and its firm refusal to yield vibrated him like pudding. Then he discovered that the tapered tip, which he could just barely reach, was so shaly with centuries of bad weather that he could crumble bits of it off in his hand. He gripped the hammer again, hitting upwards, and a block of stone the size of a man's head tumbled to the ground and rolled a few feet away. A series of shorter, quicker blows sent handfuls of gravel flying into the air. Now he could see that the interior was a mass of cracks and fissures. And with the same rhythm he had developed at the road-mending, he began to whack away large slabs with each stroke of his hammer. He continued in this fashion until the stone was a mere knob cisted to the ground.

"Well, I am pissed in the spring," he said.

*   *   *

After his success with the stone, Michael went straight to bed. Already his skull was being pierced by the first dangers of a headache and he hoped that sleep would dismiss them, though he knew they would return with a vengeance when he woke up. Fully clad, not even having bothered to remove his cap, he swathed himself in his blanket and rolled over on his belly, clamping the blanket beneath him. He thought: All honor to the fellow that invented sleep.

There came an aggressive knocking at his door just as he was starting to doze off. He wondered if it was the Guards calling about the stone. He opened the door to reveal, not the Guards, but a wet young woman with yellow frizzy hair and a notable stoop, her back weighed down by a large rucksack.

"Hi—can I come in? I'm almost drowned from all this moisture."

Michael stepped aside to let her in. She deposited her rucksack and dripping poncho on the floor.

"I was in Kinsale and I met Mary, you know, the girl from South Africa, and she told me all about you. She said I might be able to stay here, I mean, for a few days or something."

"Oh yes, Mary . . ."

"She told me all about you. You must have a really interesting lifestyle here, living off the land and all that. You see, I'm from England. Bristol. I love being in real countryside." She paused to recapture her breath. Then: "Mary said you'd be able to put me up for a while."

"Well, I don't know about that. But would you like a cup of tea?"

"Of course."

The girl's forwardness annoyed Michael. He wished she'd go away and leave him alone with his headache, a thing he was meant to suffer alone. To emphasize this, he made her tea that was as strong and black as bog water. She put the cup to her lips and grimaced right away.

"This tastes like medicine."

"That's the way we like it here. Everyone in Cahermore drinks his tea that way."

"Well, that's the way I like it, too." And she gulped bravely at the remainder of the cup, her prune-dark eyes darting about to assess the various features of Michael's digs. These eyes saw, and brightly approved, the stale specters of ten thousand meals. They returned to Michael, accompanied by a sportive grin.

"I bet I can convince you."

"Convince me of what, woman?"

"Convince you to put me up . . ."

He was not really listening to her. He was thinking about his heifer. He was thinking about no tobacco. He looked up and saw that the girl had his hand cupped between her own white, workless hands.

"Here now. What's that you're doing?"

"Convincing you . . ."

He did not take his hand away. Now the girl was leading him toward his own bedroom. This happened so quickly that he felt very remote from it, like a spectator at a film. But when he saw the girl wiggle out of her jeans, he experienced a strange flicker of desire, which came over him like a rush of feathers. For a moment, he envisioned the girl as a lush pink streak coming at him from the billowy hills around Cahermore. This image of her receded as she undid his fly. His desire, struck down at birth, fled to the mysterious place of its origin.

"We're different in our minds, you and I. But our bodies can be happy together," the girl said, climbing into bed with him. She swelled her loins and moved her knee inside his knees, trying to stir up the drowned serpent in his blood.

Her body was supple, full of a rolling grace. Michael mounted it and fumbled with it, buckrabbitting his buttocks in an effort to make some sort of union. But his old laddie wouldn't assert its ancient utility. He was facing the enemy without a spear. In the end, he tried to conjure up Maggie Mahoney, now dead, whom he had once observed dressing for Mass, her body revealed through the window in only a torn shift. Even Maggie's half-naked body would not bring back that lost feathery feeling.

The girl lay on her side, her legs curled against her belly, regarding him with a patient smile. Her yellow hair webbed her shoulders like sunlight, and he wanted to reach out and touch it. But he didn't.

"I couldn't find the rock that Mary told me about," she said, trying to make small talk.

"What rock is that?"

"You know, the one the Druids or somebody put on your land."

"That's a standing stone. But it's gone now. You've come a day too late."

The girl responded to this with a loud giggle which pounded in Michael's ears like the firing of guns. Even after she stopped, it continued to burst raucously through his head. He now felt as if she had come here just to make a mockery of him. And again he wished she'd go away, travel to Dublin, return to Bristol, go anywhere in any hemisphere, only leave him alone. For no apparent reason, he began to yearn for the soft days of glory he had shared with the South African girl Mary.

The Wrong-Handed Man

The whole world seemed to be getting divorced, so Searage decides to take his wife on a camping trip to Greenland instead. Their friends Fran and Noah have saved their marriage in Greenland. There's no pollution, says Noah. You're in the lap of nature, says Fran. What you guys need is *space*, says Noah. A marriage needs space, Fran adds, her arms resting sweetly on her pregnant belly.

"But don't hang around in Narsarssuaq," Noah tells them.

Fran: "The Army put its worst cases there during the Korean War. The soil is supposed to be paved with their ashes."

"Soil can't be 'paved' with ashes, luv," says Noah, settling into a lotus position.

Nor do Searage and his wife hang around in Narsarssuaq. Their plane lands; Searage takes a picture of an Eskimo with a "Nuke the Whales" T-shirt. And then they start clambering up the licheny rocks behind the airport. Their backpacks are not heavy. Soon they're on a plateau that reminds them of the Hindu Kush. The midnight sun bathes the landscape in a bright translucent gray. An Arctic fox comes up and sniffs at them and, as though spooked, vanishes into a cleft in the earth. They pitch their tent overlooking a flotilla of icebergs in the fjord.

"Nice view, isn't it, sweetie?"

Searage's wife is looking at the ground.

He puts his hand on her breast.

"Don't," she says, and draws away.

The next morning is nearly Mediterranean in its brilliance and sparkle. Searage emerges from their tent to find his wife slapping wildly at herself. "Damn mosquitoes . . ." she says. And in the next few minutes his own ears sing with high-pitched little squealings. "Did we bring any repellent?" he asks her.

"Fran and Noah never told us . . ."

He can hardly see his wife because of all the mosquitoes. For every one he kills, ten others jump in to take its place. His wife curses the dead little bodies floating in her granola. "Enough!" he shouts. They retreat to their tent and fasten the flap. Inside, it isn't much better.

His wife thumbs through their Baedeker. "Early missionaries. Inland ice. Transit hotels. Doesn't say anything about mosquitoes . . ." She whacks the back of his neck, rather hard, he thinks. "Four of them!" she exclaims. "I killed four of them in one blow."

He slaps her thigh. "Only three for me," he grins.

The big question is, Should they hike back to Narsarssuaq for some repellent? Or perhaps mosquito nets? Searage can't quite picture himself in the permafrost of Greenland, stuck under a mosquito net. He associates mosquito nets with their float trip down the Orinoco. Happier times. The notion of a future together. The gaily painted bodies of Indians.

"Well," he says, "what about going back to that unpronounceable human-ash place?"

"How do we even know they have bug spray there?"

Searage produces his ordnance survey map. They must be about halfway between Narsarssuaq and a small village called Igatek. He suggests they break camp now and hike on to Igatek. In Igatek, they might be able to buy bug spray. Or maybe the Eskimoes living there have their own remedy. "We might be dosed with walrus fat before the day is over," he laughs.

"Just give me one of those enormous insect bombs . . ."

They pack up their gear and start westward single file through the willow scrub and scree. According to Searage's calculation, they should reach Igatek in six or seven hours of steady walking. He puts on his stocking cap and anorak and hand-knit mittens. Whatever will protect him against the insect marauders. He puts on his North Slope snow-goggles because they shield most of his face. His wife tells him he'll be the first man ever to die of heat exhaustion in the Arctic.

No chance of that, he thinks, but he pops a salt pill anyway.

By midday they start to see a few telltale signs of civilization—spent shotgun shells, beer bottles, and a rough wooden cross cited in their Baedeker as "Possibly the grave of an Eskimo killed by polar bears." Searage gestures his wife to stand in front of the cross, no, a little to the left, so he can take a picture that will include her, the cross, and that dolomite-like peak in the distance. Smile, he says. *Smile,* he repeats. Whereupon she bursts into tears and collapses, a hurt bundle, on the ground. "It's hopeless," she tells him.

"Hopeless? What's hopeless?"

"I don't know. You, me, this whole trip. We shouldn't have come here."

"It's been less than a day . . ."

"But I don't love you anymore. I don't love you *at all* anymore. And kindly take off those silly snow-goggles. They make you look like a Sherpa."

She herself looks quite fetching with her clenched fists and tight Italian jeans, her lank auburn hair tied in a ponytail. Searage kisses her on the forehead, on a reddish mosquito bite which has appeared there like a caste mark. "Hey," he says, "Let's put down the foam mattress and let's make . . ."

"Stop. Let go of me. Please . . ." She moves crabwise away from him. Then all at once her face turns into a mask of pain. "Damn, I've just cut myself on a broken beer bottle." And she lifts her hand, palm outward, to show him the slash of blood running along her lifeline.

"I'm sorry, sweetie," he says, and takes his wife's bleeding hand gently between his mittens. With all his heart he wishes he could preserve this moment as a memory against the end of the world.

*   *   *

But now they have arrived at the end of the world. A few jerry-built houses huddle at the base of a mountain like survivors in a lifeboat. The mountain, tall and granitic, blocks off the sun. The ground is a litter of rusty tin cans and barrels and the Tinkertoy bones of seals. Here and there neat piles of stones squat among the refuse. "They don't have any soil in Igatek," says Searage, pointing to one such pile and quoting the Baedeker, "so they have to bury their dead aboveground."

"Must be fun for the dogs," his wife says.

Followed by a few grubby children, they approach a man with strong Eskimo features who is flensing a seal. Searage carefully sidesteps a mound of intestines. The seal, though dead, stares up at him with wide imploring eyes. The man smells principally of grease and urine.

"Excuse me," says Searage, speaking slowly (for that is how one speaks to natives), "but where . . . can I find . . . a doctor . . . for my wife?"

The man blows his nose through his fingers. He seems to regard them as recent visitors from outer space. A blob of mucus falls onto the seal's carcass.

"Speak any English? Parlez-vous français? Sprechen Sie Deutsch?" asks Searage's wife.

"*I* speak English." The speaker of these words is a much younger man with an International Harvester cap poised jauntily on his head. He cracks a snaggle-toothed grin and raises a beer bottle in salute. "My father is a hunter. Speaks no English. But I speak. Can I help something?"

Searage: "Well, we need a doctor. Is there a doctor here?"

"In Igatek? No doctor. Only there is a half-wife."

"Half-wife?"

"I bet he means a mid-wife," Searage's wife says.

"Yes. Woman who gets out baby. Come, I will show you."

They pick their way through the village along a path of sticky mud. Every house appears to have its own reeking midden, of which the path makes them privileged spectators. They see a little boy nearly blacked out by mosquitoes and sucking a beer bottle like a nipple. Gaunt yellowish dogs gaze at them without much apparent interest. The whole scene makes Searage think of Calcutta.

"What do you do about all these mosquitoes?" asks Searage's wife.

"Oh, we do nothing about them. How can we? They are so many, and we are few. We call them F-16's. Ha ha."

Now they come to a ramshackle house of red corrugated iron, with a slate roof. There sits an old man in front at work on some sort of carving. The man doesn't look up. "His name Sammik," says International Harvester. "It means left hand. We call this wrong hand. Wrong hand for work something. Other hand is right hand."

"Wrong Hand? Is that his name?" asks Searage.

"Yes. The Wrong-Handed One. That's Sammik. Husband of half-wife."

Inside the house, they are greeted by a bucket of seal heads. The air is redolent of musk and oily smoke, and buzzing with mosquitoes. A dead seal rests in the sink, its belly slit down the middle and the white fat peering out. They should have held your course on Death and Dying *here*, Searage whispers to his wife.

Just then an old woman comes out of the adjoining room. She is built like a perfect soapstone image of an Eskimo. Her hair is dressed in a topknot. Her eyes are narrow slits pressed deep into her head by her brow and high cheekbones. She walks like a duck full of eggs.

The woman regards first Searage, then his wife. "Gonorrhea?" she inquires politely.

"Oh no," declares Searage's wife, "It's my hand. I've cut my hand and it's bled a lot . . ."

"Can you give a tetanus shot?" asks Searage.

"Wait, wait, wait," their friend says. "This old woman, she doesn't speak English. Only one word, gonorrhea. Greenland disease. Ha ha." He exchanges a few words with the woman in a language of hisses and strangulated cries. "Show her the something," he tells them. "She will fix."

Searage's wife extends her hand. The old woman unwinds the tourniquet constructed from a strip of underwear. She puts her tongue to the wound and makes a series of sucking noises.

"She is taking out the evil spirits," their friend tells them.

"Oh Christ!" exclaims Searage.

Then the woman daubs the wound with a purplish medicine.

"Now she is putting on the iodine."

The old woman offers Searage's wife a gasoline can. International Harvester: "She must drink. Warm seal blood. Very good stuff. Half-wife say, Girl must drink this blood to put back blood she lost . . ."

"I'm not drinking *that*!"

"My wife needs a tetanus shot."

"Half-wife say she never heard of such thing."

Back outside, under the deep cerulean sky, Searage wonders whether he mightn't have imagined the whole thing. He reaches for his wife's arm, but she jerks it away. "I'm sorry, sweetie," he says, "Things aren't very up-to-date around here, that's all. I just hope it's not infected."

"And what happens if it *is* infected?"

"Well, it'll spread from place to place. Half-wife say, Vietnam will fall. Then Cambodia. Then California the Golden State."

His wife is not amused. Soon International Harvester himself joins them again, equipped with another beer. "Boat comes tomorrow. You can go to Julianehab. Plenty of doctors there. Plenty of beer, too. Ha ha."

Searage's wife: "We can arrange a flight home from Julianehab."

"Now I will meet you Sammik. Crazy old man. You can buy *tupilak* from him."

They have almost stumbled into the old man anyway. Covered with mosquitoes, he is carving at a large thighbone. He plies the wooden-handled knife in—yes—his left hand. His face is the color of hot sand and inscribed by the lineaments of bad weather. Searage is reminded of his honeymoon in Oaxaca long long ago, and of a Zapotec potter too intent upon his work to look up at the world.

International Harvester picks up a little skeletal figure, half man and half dog, carved from the nub of a reindeer horn. "We call him *tupilak.* Very strong man. First you make him come alive. Then you send him against enemy. If he doesn't kill enemy, he flies back and he kills you. He's very strong."

Searage: "Do people still believe that around here? Do *you* believe it?"

"Me? I only believe this." He grins and raises his beer bottle. "But this Sammik, he believes. He's crazy fellow. Look at him now, making atom bomb from bone of ice-bear!"

Searage looks at the figure in the old man's hand. From the shape of the bone Sammik has carved a seal and a man merged together, flippers and legs, gaping eyes. The pose is formal to the point of being hieratic. The bulging skull-plate suggests a Starving Buddha. The ribs suggest Biafra. Searage, who knows an atomic bomb when he sees one, says, "It would hardly make a dent in Hiroshima."

"Well, I think it's lovely," his wife says.

International Harvester smiles at her. "You think Igatek lovely, too?"

"We prefer Igatek to the Costa del Sol," Searage tells him. "But why do you call that thing an atomic bomb? It looks pretty much like his other figures to me . . ."

"*He* calls him atom bomb. Sammik hears on radio, Any man can make this atom bomb. He say, I am any man. I am Sammik, prima carver of *tupilaks.* I will make this something."

"He probably doesn't even know what an atomic bomb is . . ."

"Maybe. He's so old. Very, very old man. Maybe he has bad enemy which he murders. Who knows?"

Searage purchases two of the smaller *tupilaks*—a seal-dog combination with outsized flippers and something that resembles a scraggly walrus. Years from now, perhaps, they will remind him of Greenland. And the good times.

*   *   *

They have camped, on International Harvester's advice, next to a church scarcely larger than a large outhouse. Hard to imagine the whole village crowded into it. Yet, according to International Harvester, the whole village does exactly that every Sunday. Igatek likes God, my friends. And if they camp here, the children who've been trailing them everywhere will not come prying in their tent. Man and woman can get some sleep at night. Or something else. Ha ha.

Or something else.

Now as they lie side by side in their sleeping bags Searage's wife tells him she wants a divorce. I'm sure we can arrange for someone in Igatek to annul the marriage tomorrow, he replies. I can wait till we get back, she says. How's your hand, he asks. It hurts, she says. And then she falls asleep straightaway.

He sits awake listening to his own thoughts. To hear if any one of them is loud enough to speak and pierce his wife's sleep. It doesn't happen. He slips out of the tent for some fresh air and a stroll through the village.

A breeze is blowing in from the fjord. Every living creature seems to be asleep or moribund or—he looks at a skinny little dog—scratching for lice. The mosquitoes are gone: dispersed by the breeze and the chilly night.

At last I have found space, he thinks. A marriage needs space just like it needs daily supplements of seal's blood.

All at once he hears, close by, a scraping sound similar to a fingernail on a blackboard. The fingernail is being moved back and forth with a certain urgency. Then it turns into a knife. Searage has wandered into Sammik again: the Wrong-Handed Man carving away at his atom bomb in the silver-gray light of the Arctic night. As he sits down beside the old man, he feels the cartilage of excess in his own body.

"You . . . speak . . . English?"

"One English," Sammik says without raising his head. "Gonorrhea . . ."

"Well," says Searage, "it's a damn good word to know."

He stays there watching the old man work the *tupilak* into completion. The knife has a hypnotic quality. Searage finds himself possessed by a curious exhilaration, rather like the exhilaration of watching a childbirth. The man has just carved a tiny death's head in place of a navel. He gives the seal-face square teeth that stick out so far they push the lips right up to the ears. And he adds yet more ribs to the figure. In the end, Searage knows only that he must own this sculpted piece of thighbone. He thrusts seventy-five Danish crowns into Sammik's hand.

The old man, shaking his head, gives back the money.

But Searage will not be put off by an Eskimo horse-trader. He puts down another one hundred crowns. And the man gestures for him to take a carved walrus.

"I've already got one of those. I want this one. I want the atom bomb."

Fifty more crowns. Still no *tupilak*. Sammik's eyes betray no more interest than if they were contemplating a lump of rock.

Perhaps the old man really has an enemy that he wants to blow away. Well, Searage knows that money speaks louder than even homicide in these underdeveloped countries. And his money means nothing to him now. The trip is over. *Finis*. Terminated. He and his wife are, after all, going home. So he presses five hundred Danish crowns into the old man's palm. More money, he figures, than the man has ever held there in his whole hardscrabble life. "That's plenty of gonorrhea, ain't it, champ?" he says.

Sammik nods as though he understands perfectly. He grasps the completed figure with both hands and brings it to his lips. Searage can almost hear International Harvester speaking: Now Sammik is kissing this something. Now this something comes alive. Crazy old man.

Then the old man passes him the *tupilak*.

"You mean it's mine now?"

But the Wrong-Handed Man is already moving toward his house, the weight of sleep and age in his steps.

Searage heads back through the village. The horizon has turned indigo with the promise of rain. He narrowly avoids tripping over a grave mound. The stiffening wind rustles fish hung up to dry like cellophane. Tomorrow, he knows, will be a bugger. He gets to the tent just in time to save it from collapse. The pegs are useless in this wind, in the shallow ground. He weighs down the tent with stones.

"Who's there?"

"It's me, your erstwhile friend and companion. I'm coming in."

His wife looks like she's been mummified by her ArcticMaster sleeping bag. Only a little piece of her face sticks out. Her voice is bleary. "You were gone a long time."

"I paid a visit to that old man. And I bought his so-called A-bomb. You thought it was lovely, remember?"

"Yes, I remember. But go to sleep now. The boat gets here early tomorrow."

"Tomorrow," intones Searage. "Tomorrow will be a bugger."

His wife: "I'd rather have this wind than the mosquitoes."

After crawling into his sleeping bag, Searage props the *tupilak* on his chest. He stares at it for quite a while. What secrets are harbored in its ancient gaping eyes? What legends inhabit its heart of bone? What future can it foretell? Even as he is studying it, the figure appears to move its short straddling legs, beginning to walk, cautious, awake. *Reveal, O Lord! Reveal!* Searage exclaims to the figure. And suddenly the front of the tent is swept up by wind and violent rain.